the fifth

Original edition published in French under the title *Au 5e* at La Mèche, an imprint of Groupe d'édition la courte échelle inc.
Copyright © La Mèche 2017

01 02 03 04 05 25 24 23 22 21

Dagger Editions, an imprint of Caitlin Press Inc.
8100 Alderwood Road,
Halfmoon Bay, BC V0N 1Y1
daggereditions.com, caitlin-press.com

Text design by Vici Johnstone
Cover design by Derek von Essen

Printed in Canada

Caitlin Press Inc. acknowledges financial support from the Government of Canada and the Canada Council for the Arts, and the Province of British Columbia through the British Columbia Arts Council and the Book Publisher's Tax Credit.

The fifth : a love(s) story / by M.P. Boisvert ; translated by Monica Meneghetti.
Au 5e. English
Boisvert, M.P. (Marie-Pier), author. | Meneghetti, Monica, translator.
Translation of: Au 5e.
Canadiana 20200375369 | ISBN 9781773860534 (softcover)
LCC PS8603.O382 A913 2021 | DDC C843/.6—dc23

THE FIFTH

A love(s) story

by
MP BOISVERT

translated by
MONICA MENEGHETTI

Dagger Editions 2021
(an imprint of Caitlin Press)

For my godmother,
my girlfriend,
and my husband.

Quads are notoriously unstable.

—Dr. Elisabeth A. Sheff

Contents

the temporary arrangement (july)   9

    eloy   10

    alice   14

    gayle   19

    camille   23

    what was said after supper   26

    simon   33

culinary adjustments (october)   37

    gayle   38

    eloy   42

    simon   46

    what he heard   50

    camille   61

    alice   65

dark mornings (january)   69

    camille   70

    gayle   73

    eloy   77

    alice   80

    simon   83

    what she thought best to remind him   87

unchosen family (april)   97

    simon   98

    what was left unsaid   102

    camille   103

    eloy   107

    gayle   111

    alice   115

temporary arrangement—the rerun   119
(not quite july)

    alice   120

    gayle   123

    camille   125

    simon   127

    eloy   131

    what's moving   133

Translator's Note   140

About the Author   143

About the Translator   144

the temporary arrangement
(july)

eloy

getting pumped before the pizza comes

There's only one door on the fifth floor. She told me to knock but with the awful noise my VW makes, she must know I'm here.

I hate spiral staircases. Looking down at the steps makes me queasy, but if I don't look down, I trip. And carrying a box almost as wide as I am while climbing them raises the difficulty level—even though I'm not all that wide.

I had forgotten the security system on the ground floor wasn't working, so I buzzed for fifteen minutes before I tried kicking the door—my cell was dead so I couldn't call her to let me in and putting the box down didn't even cross my mind. Said door came ajar with a click that echoed the entire length of the hallway. Sigh.

My knees hurt enough already, so when I get to their door, I bend over to put the box down instead of squatting. Worst-case scenario, I put my back out and give up on moving.

No need to knock. She knows I'm here. She should have come to let me in. Clearly, she's enjoying the anticipation, tingling with the anxiety and excitement of *who knows how this will go but right now everything is still possible so please let me imagine it for a while longer.* If we were meeting at the station, she'd have her nose in a book and wouldn't look up until I cast a shadow on the pages.

I told her to give me a key. I said *it'll be easier that way, Alice.* But she insisted on being here. So she could wait for me. So I would have to knock.

There are about thirty boxes left downstairs, another batch back at the other apartment. I'm going to die. I'll die for sure. I peel my t-shirt away from my stomach and flap the material to fan myself as I go down the stairs. I look at every step this time.

I'm here because of Emily. I can still see her, crying as she did the dishes. Why can't I remember her exact words? She must have said something like *I'm leaving* because in the morning, she was gone. I definitely couldn't afford the three-bedroom on my own, even in Sherbrooke. We had to sublet. I texted Alice (*I need coffee*), we went for a beer, I wrapped up with *I don't have any furniture anyway, just a bed, everything else was hers*, and the next day, she informed me she was in talks with her room-mates about offering me a room on the fifth floor. I don't think I asked, but if I did, I must have said it would be temporary.

Sometimes I make things happen without realizing it. Maybe it was me who drove Emily to leave, in the end. Maybe she can't take all the credit for the decision. Maybe she was (finally) willing to risk living without me because she couldn't stand my apathy and detachment anymore. I think (I imagine, I suppose) she really wanted to leave, that she wanted to for a long time. But I'm pretty sure she would never have budged if it hadn't been for the rats. All those rats in the basement. I remember now: the crying-while-dishwashing incident happened after the exterminator's visit. *I can't handle it, Eloy. I can't live here anymore.*

At Alice's, there are cats instead of rats. I predict I'll get along better with them than her roomies. She avoided the subject, but I would understand them preferring someone else, anyone else. Someone who, at very least, wasn't Alice's first boyfriend (and therefore her first ex). She must have made them promises. They must have taken pity on me.

Either way, it's temporary.

I could have looked for something else, a place to myself. But this worked out too well, with the fully equipped kitchen, the furnished living room, the ridiculously low rent. A four-bedroom place isn't much space for five adults, but there's hardly any expenses. I'm here now; might as well go with it. Carry another box up, and another, and another. Fifteen round trips to the fifth.

I'd rather stay downstairs in the heat, put up with the greasy hair and dripping armpits. Hey, I'll be going up with a box when the pizza guy shows up, so he'll be forced to knock instead of me. Perfect.

Outside, there are big oak trees on either side of the entry to the building. I pick the one on the left and sit in the shade, watching my beater's hazard lights flash.

I've barely rested my back against the trunk of the tree when the building door opens. Alice has decided I need help. She so loves to anticipate my supposed needs that she came down. With iced tea.

What did I do to deserve this? She doesn't have to be so... nice.

Try as I might, I can't remember ever *wanting* to be in a situation like this. It'll go okay with Alice, despite her tendency to make sure everyone is okay all the time. As for the three others, all I know is what she was prepared to tell me. *Camille is home a lot because of her work, but she's very, very discreet. Gayle makes the best dessert in the city, just you wait. Simon can sort of get on your nerves about cleaning, but just stick to the chore schedule and it'll be fine....*

I'll put up with them. Which doesn't mean respect will follow.

She'll sit down. I'll sigh. She'll smile at me. I'll look down and drink my iced tea, resist the urge to pour the pitcher over my head, thank her, carry some more boxes.

She sits closer to me than I would have liked, but first she takes the time to get comfortable by spreading a picnic blanket on the lawn.

You didn't knock is what she says, brow furrowed, while handing me a glass.

She's a funny one. She thinks things happen like they do in her head, where I'm here and we're *friends*. She's always wanted that, for us to *be friends*. I feel bad, asking this much of her. She probably thinks I'm not asking enough, that I'm mean, insensitive—yeah, that's it, insensitive. I'm living here until. Until I find something better.

I think about it all the time. I try to be patient—I try way too hard—and usually succeed. And sometimes when I start thinking about it, I panic.

I finally force out a response: *Hello, Alice.*

She smiles. *You're a cute one, you. Everything okay?*

No, it's not, but I don't say that. No big deal, this too shall pass.

I go to drink the iced tea, but my aim is off. I pour it all through my beard.

alice

For the third time since the sun decided to wake me up at six o'fucking clock in the morning, winning the war with curtains I should've replaced a long time ago, the no-pressure shower head trickles glacial water down the length of my back.

I sigh with contentment.

It's not quite nine and everyone else is still asleep—except Gayle, as per yoozh. Eloy's not here yet. I'm back in the shower because I'm hot. The living room is just as much of a sauna as my bedroom. The timid gush of chilly water reminds me I'm intelligent and intelligible; a human being, not a walking dishrag.

Might as well stay in here. Cold water is practically free, and who cares if my teeth are chattering? My knees were already shaking anyway.

His arrival—*more like "his return"*—reminds me there was a time when I tried having Just One™. One at a time. Like you're supposed to. I'd forgotten.

I'd paired up with Just One™, a Monogamous-but-not-Monosexual, and I was one of those too, or I thought I was. I thought we were two of a kind. We were head-over-heels, it was True Love. Head-over-heels, as in *words can't express how much I love you, people* say *they're in love but they have no clue what it means because no one could* possibly *love each other as much as we do, other people are doing it wrong, other people are losers.*

It was hopeless. Our love snobbery oozed from every pore.

And then, shenanigans. Someone else came along and I fell head-over-heels again—a different head-over-heels of course, but no less intense, so I wanted them both and tried to have them both. Without telling them. What a great idea.

Soon, instead of having Just One™ times two, I had none at all. You can't mess with the trademark, but I didn't understand that yet.

Even worse, the second one wasn't up to par. Actually, people were always reminding me of it. That he wasn't worth the trouble. As if I didn't know.

My hair doesn't need washing, but I tip my head back and wet it anyway just to take the cold with me when I get out, to keep it on my head a little longer. My skin dries too fast.

Whether it's a novel or a film, it's always the same: you're supposed to choose. You absorb that. *I* absorbed that. I thought I needed the ease of a relationship and the excitement of cheating. All I had to do was not mention my partners to anyone. That's how it is in the fairy tales. I just had to do the same in real life. I wish I could say I read the wrong stories, but the right ones, the ones suited to my endless supply of love, weren't exactly available. That's always the problem, the lack of available options. That and limited time: you can't read *all* the stories.

The ultimate curse.

I debate whether to wash because I already did, just after I was forced out of bed. I have no problem with the feel or smell of my own sweat. I only took a shower because I couldn't take the heat anymore but since I'm here, I might as well soap up again. I have nothing else to do but think....

...Oh, wait, Eloy did this too, just before we met for the first time. He took three showers before I got to his place, to escape his parents and little brother. It was the only way of getting any peace and quiet in their little house in Saint-Eustache, he told me later. That was before his parents went back to Témiscamingue, before we were old enough to see each other without them breathing down our necks. He also told me, when I questioned his choice of wearing jeans in that heat, *I don't wear shorts.*

Maybe I shouldn't have insisted he come live with us. Nostalgia, pity, all that shit—they got the better of me. He said he was looking for a place *just for a few months, just until I find a job* and already the next day, I was discussing it with the fifth floor Family.

No, I shouldn't have insisted because now if it backfires, it'll be my fault. But really, how could it go wrong? He's not judgy, he understands, he wants to fit in, I just know it, even though he never said it in so many words.

But it's not like he's the most transparent guy, so maybe I shouldn't put my faith in him. Too late, he's on his way here. There will be a bed in his room, another towel in the bathroom and another place at the table. There will be five of us. Too bad. Four's a good number, a square number, literally. Four corners, four sides. Although we're less a square than a triangle with a line extending from one of the corners that's kind of unrelated to the rest—a nameless polygon.

Four was good, but I'm incapable of saying no to someone I love. Or rather, used to love. Someone I loved a little less over time. Well, not really *less* but differently. Actually, I never really stopped loving him. So, I still love him, but not in the same way, you know?

I couldn't say no. Plus, he fits in well. He will fit in well. Just have to give him some time.

No matter how much I concentrate on each swipe of soap over my body's endless peaks and valleys, I can't help thinking about him moving in—angsting, that is, over the concept of him being here. Showers are too routine. I should have taken a bath, balanced a computer on the lid of the toilet to watch a movie, but that would have meant cleaning the tub—too much work. I was hot. Still hot, actually.

He's not even here yet and I'm already imagining the in-verted triangle of sweat on the back of his t-shirt. If it weren't against the law, I'd definitely be topless while helping him with his boxes—it's so unfair. I could always encourage him to take *his* shirt off instead—*It's legal for you, so why not take advantage?*—even though he'd never take it off willingly. No one should ever glimpse his skeletal body carrying boxes, those non-existent muscles flexing under milky-white skin.

And yet, I find him attractive. Okay, the last thing I need is to start fantasizing. I'm hot enough already.

I finish by soaping my crack, fishing out the stray hairs that washed down my back and lodged there when I was wet-ting my head earlier. The clump of hair doesn't go down the drain. I stick it to the tiles, hoping I don't forget it there.

The iced tea must be ready, but if I get out of the shower, I run the risk of bumping into Simon and being assailed by his judgments—*you're too nice to him* or *so, when are you going to sleep with him?* or, best-case-scenario, *eww! Where'd you find that towel?* Might as well give it a shot anyway. Maybe Simon will still be in his room and Camille will sleep until ten.

Even though we try hard to keep the place cool by keeping the windows shut and running the portable air conditioner, the kitchen is humid with the scent of freshly baked cookies. Gayle greets me with a sticky hug that I want to disentangle from ASAP—with both of us wearing undershirts, our arms slide against each other, as greasy as the cookie sheets. Still, I'm grateful. In her arms, I may drip sweat but being there calms me.

I'm so excitedly anxious, I'll jump ten feet in the air if he knocks right now. Gayle opens the fridge and hands me the iced tea. I lean over it and stir, arrange everything on the tray and taste again: perfect. I'll go back outside and wait for him like a groupie. I'll sit on the garden wall with my legs crossed and everything. Cute, eh?

Simon's waiting to be proven right, I just know it—*It didn't go well with the last cis-dude roomie, I don't see how this guy would be any different.* I know Eloy is Simon's type, even if he'd never admit it—when I showed him a photo of Eloy, he swallowed funny. I shouldn't try to convince or comfort Simon. He doesn't need to hear how good looking and nice Eloy is either, so don't mention it. Don't enable.

If they wind up sleeping together, I can brag about sparking some slash fiction between my ex-boyfriends. If Simon knew that had crossed my mind—even if it was just for a fraction of a second, tops—would he hold it against me?

gayle

eating breakfast before everyone else

I don't know what got into me, baking cookies in this heat. I wound up eating a ton. So, even if I tell them *I only ate one, had to make sure they were good*, they probably won't buy it because now I'm not hungry so if Alice decides to make crêpes, I won't be eating any. Fuck off. At least Camille won't comment on it; she'll just be happy I made dessert.

Hello, my name is Gayle, and I'm a cookie-holic.

Alice is freaking out this morning. She's been in the bathroom for, like, an hour. I thought my cookie-brunching was going to be hard to hide, but I had plenty of time to make the dough, scoop them onto the sheet, bake them, and let them cool for thirty seconds before eating...one, two, three, four, seven. Seven empty circles on the cookie sheet.

Oops.

I'll put the rest into the cookie jar right away, so no one will be able to count what's left.

I like being alone in the kitchen. That way, no one can accuse me of overeating for a while, except me. Although that's also precisely the advantage to there being four of us: I can't go seriously overboard, since everyone's aware of what's in the fridge.

Oh right, there'll be five of us soon, Eloy gets here this morning! How exciting!

I'm glad I'm not the hinge this time. When Raphael was here, I felt responsible for him, and when things got messed up, I felt a bit bad, like it was my fault. I suppose it kind of was. Everything was okay until I told Simon *I'm sure he thinks you're cute, he just doesn't know how to broach it. Make the first move.* Only to later find out that when Simon *did* come on to him, Raph spit in his face. Not a very polite way of saying *I'm not interested.* Insulting, even. We had to kick him out after that, otherwise Simon would've moved out, and Alice right along with him, and voilà! Nobody left on the fifth floor.

It turned out Raph loved everything about sex, as long as it didn't violate the one-dick rule. I figured that out a bit late, when I realized he considered Camille my *boy*friend (while still finding her attractive, what the fuck?) and in spite of that he said *I just can't picture it, you know?* No, I didn't know, and I hadn't asked for his opinion. He gave it to me anyway.

For all I know, he probably even thought my sex life with Alice was lacking a little "je ne sais quoi" since a dick is apparently essential for pulling off a fuck fest.

So yeah, kind of my fault, that massive fail, because I didn't "investigate" him. We took our breaks at the same time at work, on the third floor of that glass monstrosity at the corner of Frontenac and Belvédère. He was into contemporary dance—a rare thing at the Ministry of Education. He invited me to a Pina Bausch performance, and we had a great time. I told him about my little Family of roommates. His questions were fairly to-the-point: *So, Alice is your girlfriend, but she's also with Simon? Doesn't it bother him to share?* All smiles, I explained how it's best not to speak in terms of "sharing" because it implies that he owns her. Sweetheart.

He was looking for a place to live and wouldn't you know it, we had a room available!

After the face-spitting incident, Simon didn't speak to me for quite a few weeks and Alice stopped sleeping with me and Camille.

Ever since then, we have four rules for roomies:

1. The person must be a long-standing acquaintance (length at the discretion of whichever of us knows them);
2. The Family's romantic situation must be made explicit to them from the outset;
3. They must have no history of face-spitting (non-consensually);
4. Any queerphobic remark, innuendo, or joke will result in immediate eviction.

Oh Alice, my Alice! Come get your iced tea, don't mind me... Did you do all that for Eloy, that beautiful tray with our best glasses? Fancy much? Please Lord, don't let her count the cookies. Come on, sweetie, don't try to avoid me, I'm going to hit you full force with this smile. See my grin brimming with subtext? It says *I find these circumstances so absurd, but I know it's not funny to you, my poor baby. I love you and will support you from afar because I love looking at you, and watching you get all embroiled. Will you sleep in my room tonight? I want you to tell me all about it.*

I've been wanting Alice to sleep in our room again—Camille's and my room—for quite a while now because sleeping three to a bed is fucking great, aside from the fact that one of us inevitably winds up in the middle, dying of heat. Simon and Alice have gotten into the habit of sleeping in his room, which

I can't for the life of me understand—I love him well enough, but he snores like a trucker.

How do I put this? The four of us have found a balance that's pretty hard to achieve when you're in Relationship Type X in a world full of Type Y relationships.

The harmony we've achieved throws all the nay-sayers for a loop.

And now, Eloy comes along and, like Simon said when Alice was trying to convince us, *how do we know he won't ruin everything?*

Actually, there is no way to know what impact this newbie will have on the Family. Even though Alice knows him well. Even though he seems tidy enough. Even though he's good looking. Even though he's nice.

How long will we be able to put up with him? With each other? How long before we find the new normal?

I like change, but not this much.

At least it's an excuse to make cookies. I'm stress-baking. All this potential drama! It's worthy of a lot of Chipits and brown sugar.

But what if my cookies aren't any good?

Maybe I should have another one. Or two. Just to be sure.

camille

getting fed up in front of a clean plate

We were here first.

It doesn't bother me that much really, Whatshisname moving in. I'm the most adaptable, shall we say. But I need my space. Space to think. About myself. Because I only just started to *become* myself. To become *her.*

Because there have been a few Camilles in my life, but never one like Camille Bergeron from the sitcom *Radio Enfer.* That Camille was me. No one could convince me otherwise.

Camille Bergeron hated makeup. She played ringette and passed the time reading and pushing her glasses back up on her nose. She was in love with Leo Rivard, the technical director, who also was a bit like me, but the boy version of me, the me I would have been if my body had been right for me.

Camille understood me. Like me, she had to learn how to be "a real girl," the kind of girl people expected her to be, so they wouldn't be suspicious of her. You can be whoever you want on the inside and no one questions it until the day you decide to wear a skirt, so you better know how to play the role.

Clothes are a serious matter.

Eloy moving in makes me think back to the very beginning, when Alice was trying to convince us—Gayle and me—that living with Simon could be a good idea. She had a vision, she called it, of having a house with a cubby hole under the stairs where we could store all my tights, *just like at your grandmother's where all the toys were*. She said it often (*you'll be able to dress however you want, you'll see*). But despite her urging (*why not take advantage of it to buy yourself some skirts?*), I didn't believe I could get on top of dressing appropriately at the time, much less move out of my mom's place—yes, even at my age. I may be adaptable, but that doesn't mean I'm independent.

Okay, so we didn't find that place with a cubby hole under the stairs for hiding my tights (the only stairs are the ones leading up to the apartment, not exactly ideal). I just wore tights occasionally at first. When I was alone. Sometimes when I was with Gayle. Or Alice. Or both of them. I wore them under my pants. Then I started wearing them with a skirt. With a bra. Without a bra. And now I wear them all the time.

We've been at the table for at least an hour. Forty-five minutes since we finished eating lunch and Alice is still blabbing away, mostly because no one else wants to talk. I don't bat an eye since, theoretically, I'm a good girl, very well-behaved, even though I have the urge to be a bit naughty, just so I get punished. Argh, better not think about that. I'm wearing my tight hipster jeans, so if I think about spankings, it'll show.

Can't say the new arrival is very amusing so far. He's looking down, arms crossed. Me, I want some fun. I want to jump onto my bed and get jumped. It's so simple. And much more entertaining. I wouldn't get sick of *that* going on for an hour.

When Alice finishes lecturing us, I can roleplay the Maid. Once we get to the part where we *do* the housework instead of *talking* about it, I can titillate Gayle with a French Maid costume and no underwear. I won't be able to actually put it on, not in front of Eloy—same problem as with the tights, okay, whatever, fine—but I can allude to it at least.

(I'm always thinking about it. About being taken, being devoured, being treated like a plaything. It's all I want to be used for. Thinking is hard. I only think because I have to, but when I'm in my Mistress's arms, she does the thinking for me. I love it. I want to be looked after.)

Oh, sorry for not listening, Alice, but don't blame me, blame your chest.

Simon is punishing me with his eyes—I know, honey, I'm so uncivilized.

I have trouble with strangers, and if this trend continues, soon there will be what, six, seven, thirty-four, a thousand of us? Always because of Alice. She's trying to make me sociable! Me, someone who puts so much effort into withdrawing from the world, into going unnoticed so I can dedicate myself entirely to role play! I'm going to be assimilated. All because she can make me do anything she wants, just by pinching my nipple and grabbing my crotch.

I can't wait to see what'll happen with the new guy. He doesn't seem all that insignificant to me.

Ugh, does this mean I won't be able to scream as loud?

I'll get Gayle to gag me.

what was said
after supper

Eloy's room.

Drawn curtains, dim light. Stacks of boxes and green garbage bags cover the floor. Eloy, wearing a navy-blue hoodie and faded black slim-fit jeans, holds a bag open with one hand while pulling t-shirts out of it with the other.

Camille appears at the half-open door. She's dressed in hiking shorts and a sports bra.

CAMILLE *smiling, one hand on the doorframe and the other on her hip*
>Hey.

ELOY *keeping his head down*
>Hey.

CAMILLE
>The door was open. Thought you might need some help.

ELOY *keeps pulling clothes out of the bag and laying them on the bed*
>I'm good, you don't have to.

CAMILLE

I know I don't have to, but I feel like helping you.

ELOY

Really, it's not necessary.

CAMILLE

Yeah, I know you're a big boy. But I don't have anything better to do.

Eloy sighs.

Camille imitates his sigh.

ELOY

'kay.

CAMILLE

Great. What were you doing?

ELOY

Taking my clothes out of bags.

CAMILLE

How thrilling. What can I do?

ELOY

Well...put them away, if you want.

She picks up a t-shirt riddled with holes around the neck, and raises an eyebrow.

CAMILLE

As you wish!

Twenty minutes elapse, during which Camille silently judges the wardrobe emerging from the bags.

Eloy suddenly turns toward Camille.

ELOY *croaks out, as though his voice were changing*
So...

CAMILLE
Yeah?

ELOY *abruptly switching to a near whisper*
What do people call you?

CAMILLE *unwavering*
Camille!

Eloy focuses on the belt he's holding and pulls on the buckle with his index and third finger, testing its strength.

ELOY
I know, but... you know what I mean.

CAMILLE
Not really, no.

ELOY
What do people use? To call you?

CAMILLE *turning toward him*
A telephone?

ELOY *defeated by Camille refusing to play along*
Pronouns, Camille. What pronouns do you use?

CAMILLE *proudly*
I, you, she, he, we, us, they!

ELOY

For fuck sakes!

CAMILLE

Jesus! Why so serious? I use "she." I tried using "they," but it tripped me up, even though I do find it pretty cute. If you ever get it wrong, just apologize and move on.

Eloy, holding a small box, weaves around all the bags to get to his computer, which is balanced on top of a pile of books on his desk. He pulls a pair of speakers out of the box, plugs them into the computer and opens iTunes.

Another twenty minutes go by while clothes get folded and music plays.

CAMILLE *shoulders slumped, having lost some of her aplomb*

What about you? What's your deal, honey?

ELOY

My what?

CAMILLE

Your thing. Your preferences.

ELOY *imitating Camille's earlier sarcasm*

In music? Books? Films?

CAMILLE

Your *sexual* preference, Eloy.

ELOY

Oh my God! I had *no clue* that's what you meant.

CAMILLE

You're cute when you're being sarcastic.

ELOY

I'm into women.

Silence for about thirty seconds, punctuated by the sound of Eloy rummaging through boxes.

CAMILLE

Define "woman."

ELOY *looks up, ruffled*

Uh-oh.

CAMILLE

At least you didn't say you were into *girls*. That would've been worrisome....

Silence.

Camille bounces her crossed leg. Eloy sits in his computer chair to unpack some office supplies and put them in his desk.

CAMILLE

You're not into men at all?

ELOY

Not really, no.

Total silence.

ELOY *scratches his beard noisily and mumbles*

What about you? Have you been with a guy before?

CAMILLE

A few times.

ELOY

>   And?

CAMILLE

>   It was nice, I'd say. That's about all. I can't put "gold-star lesbian" on my resume, but I have more glorious achievements.

ELOY

>   Hm.

CAMILLE

>   Why? Interested?

ELOY

>   Nah. I'd rather have a virgin ass.

CAMILLE *gets up to leave*

>   If you only knew.

ELOY

>   Oh, come on, I was joking!

CAMILLE *heading for the door*

>   It wasn't funny. You know the rules.

Eloy reaches out as if to keep her from leaving, then shrinks back once he catches sight of his outstretched hand.

Camille is looking at him, her brow furrowed.

ELOY *crossing his arms*

>   It slipped out. I was just fooling around. I thought you'd get that.

CAMILLE *hesitating*

How would I know you were being ironic? I hardly know you.

ELOY
    It won't happen again.

Silence.

Camille sits down again.

ELOY *smiling for the first time*
    At least not for a day or two.

CAMILLE *in a scolding tone*
    You're a real shit disturber.

ELOY *smiling even wider*
    No, as I was just saying!

Satisfied sneer. Camille flings a t-shirt in his face and dashes out.

ELOY *shouting after her*
    Oh, c'mon! That was a good one!

simon

alone in a crowded house

I'm not your babysitter. Since when don't you want me hanging out with people from the university? I already made plans, deal with it, she said, and left. As though it were a night like any other. She's never here when I need her. I don't know what she was thinking, leaving us here with him when we don't even know each other. He could set the place on fire, for all we know, just for the fun of it.

Okay, fine, he wouldn't do that. He knows it would hurt him. *Whatever happens, no harm must come to him.*

I heard them giggling over there. Folding clothes is just another excuse to flirt. He just got here and already he's stirring shit up.

They don't know I can see them. I'm positioned perfectly, you see. My room is right in front of his. I watch him pick up his boxes one by one. Grab his bags, one by one. Pick them up and open them. Reach inside and pull out his stuff. A bedside lamp. A pencil case. A book.

Argh, I can't make out the title. I'll have to go snoop once he leaves. *Tell me what you read, and I'll tell you who you are.*

I'm going to stay in my room all evening, deprive myself of enjoying my own couches to avoid him. Lunch was enough of a welcome, watching him squirm, trying to make him even more uncomfortable. It's my place, I'll do what I want.

Our rooms are too close together, that's the problem. We need a house, not this minuscule apartment.

I'd forgotten he was so good looking. It unsettles me. It's unsettling.

An ex isn't like everyone else.

There's something between you and an ex.

That is, there *was* something between you. Fucking, to be exact. Alice and Eloy were together for eight months, after all. In high school, eight months is an eternity. They slept together; Alice even said they particularly enjoyed *doing it*—isn't that charming. Anyway, it's the sort of relationship that you're supposed to lock away in the darkest recesses of your brain.

But no, not Alice. Alice never lets anyone go.

She talked to me about him on our second date—as if you do that, talk about your ex when you're trying to seduce each other. I was twenty-one, I'd never had a girlfriend (or a boyfriend, for that matter). She explained their breakup had been hard, but she'd gotten back in touch with him after a few months—she added him on Facebook on a whim; it was easy, so easy! So much easier than it had been when they were teenagers (nothing is easy when you're a teenager).

Our second date, and I was already in love. I couldn't figure out how I'd never really *seen* her, even though she'd been right there all along—the best friend of my best female friend for all of high school, the one who went to another school. I'd seen her twice at Andrea's, boring parties where I would hunch in the corner criticizing all the insipid things everyone would say. A stereotypical Sherbrooke soap opera, bourgeois-style.

Her talking about him on our second date didn't faze me at all. He was an ex—no competition. He'd had his chance. She'd shown him the door before I came along, so he was nothing to her. Less than me.

Four years later, I'm the one who's the ex. Less than him.

Two years ago, she wanted me back in her life because I had changed, because she was with *them*, Gayle and Camille, and I was no longer associated with disappointment, inner turmoil, depression—or passion, even. Now if she wants *him* back in her life, he'll become my equal and take over my position as the most recent addition to the Family. And even though she's already experienced New Relationship Energy, I know it will sweep her away again because yes, that horror show can happen again, the flame can re-ignite. When she looks at those two, *the girls*, with her combination of sweetness and solicitousness, it makes me smile. But the idea of her looking at *him* that way nauseates me. Why is that? I have no idea.

Finding him attractive doesn't help.

He's here to stay, that's obvious. He says it's temporary but he's already getting attached. And I get it. These women are the loves of my life and they're out of this world, their very existence is impossible. And when you find them—*ah, when you find them*—you cling to them like you never knew was possible. He's already there. His second day here, and he's already fallen in love. Just like me on that second date.

I've seen him—escaping into the cats' fur, holing up in his room with the door shut, pretending the food isn't as good as it is.

I've seen him—looking out the window for another place like this, checking to see if the outside world still exists, trailing his fingertips along the walls as he walks down the hallway to reassure himself they're really there.

I don't see how we're so different. Why she would need two of her exes instead of just one.

Both of us: exes.

He will sit in *my* armchair, piss in *my* toilet, turn on *my* lights, drink from *my* glasses. He's going to mess everything up. Everything. I'm going to stay in my room, it's better that way.

It would be better if he stayed in his room, too. Definitely.

culinary adjustments
(october)

gayle

baking brownies

Okay, so, this goes where? he asks.

The sweetie.

He'd much rather not ask, open all the cupboards and figure out on his own where to put the colander, except he knows I'll quirk an eyebrow if he does that in front of me.

I'm so into him.

We have nothing in common, nothing to talk about. He's not my usual type, more the spitting image of Simon's dream guy, who hasn't mentioned it, by the way, even though he's drooling all over himself. But it's true, I do find Eloy attractive, and judging by the way he checks me out when he thinks I'm not looking, he finds me not half bad either. I don't agree with him—he'd change his mind if he saw me braless—but I appreciate the attention. I don't feel like *touching* him, but I do get the urge to hug him. We have nothing in common, and I don't care. I'm into him.

He offers to do my cake-baking dishes now, without fail. I'm not sure if he's doing it to encourage me to bake cakes more often, to be polite, or just because he's bored. Most likely it's because he wants to be near the oven when the timer dings so he can be the first to taste whatever buttery, chocolatey, brown-sugary concoction emerges.

I'm so into him. Like my grandmother said to my mother's boyfriend after meeting him for the first time: *You're quiet and you do dishes: you can come back anytime.*

Tonight, I opted for Rocky Roads. I haven't made them since he moved in, but it should be a hit, because, I mean, it's basically brownies topped with marshmallows, walnuts, and a caramel drizzle. A fucking delicious caramel drizzle I made from scratch. Check me out, stirring it with my big wooden spoon.

While he scrubs the pans with the green and yellow sponge, hair falls in front of his eyes. Maybe it'll prompt him to ask me to cut it for him.

Last Wednesday, it was just the two of us for dessert night. It totally undid him, craving what was hidden in the oven so much while pretending not to care. He'd made the mistake of leaving his bedroom door open—the mouth-watering scent made him easy prey—and he eventually turned up in the kitchen while I was licking the bowl, catching me in the act. I must have jumped ten feet. He realized (finally) that I was susceptible, which he found either reassuring or unsettling, but either way, he got right down to washing the huge pile of dishes always left in the wake of a buttery, chocolatey, brown-sugary delight. That night, I was the one to put the dishes away. Neither of us said a word.

When the peeps got back and found the kitchen spotless, they must have been confused.

Rocky Road brownies are a bit like the Cadillac of desserts. And apparently, from the way Eloy's looking at my caramel, I've hit the spot. I don't know what got into me. He seemed a bit bored (as usual), but also a little worked up (not usual), so I just said, *so, why aren't you and your girlfriend together anymore?* and he fell apart in front of me so fast, I thought he'd fall to the floor, the poor thing went soft as a marshmallow. I must have said *I'm sorry* twenty-five times in three seconds, *ack! Sorry, I didn't mean to say that, sorry, I'm sorry, I'm so sorry, I shouldn't have asked, it's none of my business,* all of it punctuated with his *it's okay, it's okay, really, it's okay,* followed by a long silence.

To make up for it (this girl's no idiot), I handed him a beer, pushed out a chair, and he just nodded, sat down, took the bottle, downed half of it in one swig and voilà, I was back to being the nice dessert-making roomie, even though he still looked gloomy.

Emily found me hard to live with.

How bizarre.

He adds: *She was hard to live with too. She didn't need me.*

You don't have to talk about it, I say again, *sorry, I didn't mean to pry.*

He half-smiles.

Why do you apologize all the time?

This guy's no idiot.

Sorry for apologizing?

He takes another big gulp of beer, drums his fingers on the table. He doesn't look at me and I don't know what to say although I'm liking the way he's opening up to me. How long before he clams up again?

Do you find us *hard to live with?*

Oh, I saw that little smile, I haven't lost you yet, super babe.

No, except when it's Camille's turn to cook.

Legit.

He chuckles.

Do you still talk to her?

Who, Camille?

No, your ex.

Ah. No.

It must have been a bad breakup from the looks of things. Still, I've always had trouble understanding how people can cut off contact like that, *bang!*, after sharing love, sex, and bills for years. All that intimacy gone, poof, just like that. The semi-closure, the utter sadness of it.

What are you doing tomorrow?

Sending out CVs.

Oh yeah? Where to?

I don't know, just...out.

The job market here's supposed to be shitty.

That it is.

Hm.

In ten minutes flat, we've managed to talk about his love life, his job situation, and his future. That should hold us for a while, eh?

eloy

advancing the cause of tofu

I'm not sure what they want from me.

When I have to be in the kitchen, they all take advantage of it. Maybe they're hoping I'll entertain them. They even manage to find something to do in exactly the same place, at exactly the same time, so they can hang around me. And yet I'm just cooking, not stripping.

I don't know what's so fascinating about me, apart from being younger, skinnier, and hairier than them—and possibly more educated too, although I doubt they're looking to be reminded of that.

Sometimes I even manage to be funny. But only if someone deserves it, and no one here is worthy. Especially not me.

I trip over the small cat while going to throw broccoli into the wok. He was lying on the floor right behind me while I was cutting the florets into more or less bite-sized pieces. If I hadn't been told not to, I would pick him up with my left hand while carrying the cutting board in my right to balance it out. The amount of cat hair in the food dramatically increased since my arrival, so a new rule has been instituted: *No cat-holding while cooking.*

It's a pain in the ass. If one of them rubs up against my legs, how am I to refuse? Does he not deserve special attention, a perfect score for his dignified bearing? Should he meow to express his needs, am I supposed to ignore him on the grounds of a rule meant to prevent the proliferation of fur even though it's in the very air we breathe and blankets every surface?

It's so arbitrary. Not letting me pet the cats as I please is their way of controlling me. Of punishing me for being in their natural habitat.

Speaking of punishment, I heard them again last night.

I don't think Simon was with them. From what I can tell, the "sleeping" arrangements change every night, mostly according to Alice's mood and libido. She spends at least one night a week in each room—except mine, of course.

So, then it must have been just them, the women. I heard the sound of a hand (or hands) smacking skin—which area(s) of skin, I have no idea—and breathless murmuring, muffled moans, stifled cries.

I'm not sure how I feel about it.

I considered pounding on the dividing wall so as not to keep all the awkwardness to myself. I thought about putting in earplugs, but I only had Q-tips and was afraid they'd get stuck. I considered sleeping in the living room, but I probably would have heard just as much out there and been physically uncomfortable as well.

More uncomfortable than right now, which is saying a lot.

I'm not sure what's behind this awkwardness I feel. Is it longing? Disgust? Amazement? Am I turned on? Alice and I were just kids when we were a thing. Sixteen-year-old kids, but still kids. Strange times. Maybe I wanted to spank her back then, or tie her up, ask her to call me Sir. Maybe I just didn't know it yet.

In this apartment, love and sex are everywhere. All four of them snuggle up together at the slightest provocation, no matter how banal. Say Alice runs into Camille on the way to the bathroom. They will hold each other for ages. Or say Gayle joins Alice and Simon on the couch to watch a movie. She will sit between them and get lovingly enveloped. Only Simon refuses cuddles when offered, and sometimes Alice. No one seems to mind.

Me, I only cuddle the cats, and they even cuddle me back. They're softer anyway.

I asked that we eat less meat. Three months of cooking vegetarian when it's my turn. Camille is the only one who still seems put off by tofu, which I'm currently stir-frying in the wok. Meanwhile Simon is always making us eat venison steak: *My dad hunted for it himself, so it doesn't count!*

If they aren't trying to get at me, why are they hanging around me right now? Simon always stays as far away from me as possible, as though I have the plague; Alice always stays closest, as though hoping for something from me.

I don't know what I think of all this yet. If I said something like that to Alice, she'd say: *How can you not know?*

She comes up close to the wok, and therefore me, and I just know she's holding back from telling me to tie my hair back.

Can I help?

That's her main question, every day.

I'm good.

She's going to ask again, wait for it…

Are you sure?

Ha!

I'm sure.

I wait for her to move away before turning around to grab the carrots off the table. She takes refuge in Simon's arms, who immediately buries his nose in her hair.

Gayle chatters away, just to fill the silence: *Ooh, smells so good! What sauce do you put on it? Tofu is so good, how come I never ate it before this summer? I gotta say, my parents aren't big on cooking anything besides omelettes and overcooked spaghetti, so you know, even though I haven't lived with them for a long time, I haven't strayed far from their ways, food is such a traditional thing, eh? It's tough to change. Anyway, I'm happy to eat anything that's not reheated microwave french fries nowadays, I love my parents, okay? But that's just kind of sad. Hey, that reminds me, we'll be out of cat food soon, should go buy some, I would've gone today but I didn't think of it until after five and the pet store was already closed, have to remember to go tomorrow, I'll send you all a reminder on our WhatsApp group, if it comes to that. Is tomorrow already Wednesday? Um, no, it's Tuesday, so I think you'll have to be the one to get it, Cam. Should think about bringing the plants inside too, especially the herbs. It's starting to get cold at night.*

I scoop the stir-fry onto plates, happily imagining how the cats will relish the scent of all this basil.

simon

I'm not especially picky or bourgeois. I was just raised on good meat. Meat cooked to shoe leather will never enter my mouth. I like it fresh and tender, occasionally from frozen but always cooked to perfection.

It's because of my parents. Birthday dinners with them are always raclette, and raclette always involves venison. With spices that cost thirty-five dollars a jar.

(Yeah, okay, maybe it *is* a little bougie.)

I really wish I could grill these on the barbecue, but I hate having to light the thing. Alice is the one who usually takes care of that—Alice takes care of everything around here—and she's still out, so frying pan it is. Too bad.

Sometimes I wish she had fewer friends, fewer places to go, less work to manage. She's always out yet expects us to always be home. Especially me. As if I had nothing better to do (well, I kind of don't, do I?). As if I were here for her pleasure. Camille can fantasize all she wants, I'm the maid around here.

Is "maid" gender-neutral?

If it were just the two of us living here, I'd make cheese scones and wait for her, wearing nothing but an apron. She would come through the door, see me, let out a lustful moan and suggest I hop up onto the counter, then give me the blowjob of the century.

But I will do no such thing. She doesn't deserve it. It shouldn't bother me that she's not here. I should be happy that she went out if she felt like it. Camille and Gayle went with her. They wanted a girls' night out. I grumbled, not wanting to be left behind. Alice said *we're not excluding you, my love, we just want some time to ourselves.*

So, the steak will be for the two of us, Eloy and me. An imposed guys' night in. Whatever that is.

This it too much venison for two people. He'll point that out, I'm sure. *Too much meat, not enough salad* he'll say, and I'll say *there was only a tiny bit left in the fridge,* and he'll say *you could have gone to get some.*

And he's right, I could have gone for some and gotten out a bit myself. Doing groceries never hurt anyone, right? Well, as long as you don't bump into my mother, who adds twenty-five frozen things to my basket because she's afraid I'm not eating enough, then offers to pay while mentioning yet again that I should be saving to buy a house rather than renting: *It's like throwing money out the window, you know, you should invest!*

Changing grocery stores would be a stellar plan.

We have celery and carrots, I'll cut them up for crudité so he won't hassle me.

Or not. I shouldn't give a shit about him; after all, he doesn't give a shit about me. Last week, when it was his turn to cook, he made scalloped potatoes and I spent the night writhing in pain. An entire meal laden with cream and cheese for lactose-intolerant me. Thanks, Eloy, thanks so much. It was really good but not worth the trouble (*that's what they said*).

Since he got here, things have changed.

There are wine glasses in a cabinet that doesn't match the décor.

There's someone in the shower at 7:30.
There's canned soup in the pantry.

He came into the kitchen when my back was turned. I heard the fridge open. I'm tired and lost in thought and must be confused because I just said *could you set the table,* babe*?* But I didn't mean to say "babe," it just slipped out....

My ears are red and I feel sick. Stay focused on the steak. Is the meat cooked properly? I should add more salt and pepper. They're on the table, so I would have to turn around but he's there, *setting the table*, doing what I asked, even though I was talking to someone else. To "babe."

When I finally do turn around, he's set out two placemats, two plates, two sets of utensils, two goblets. There's a bottle of red wine in the centre of the table. A cat in his arms.

I didn't expect the wine. I hate not being informed ahead of time what's going to happen.

What are we going to say to each other for a whole bottle of wine?

Looks good.

Okay, that's a start.

It's nothing.

Can I do something?

No, the only thing left is peeling the potatoes.

I'll pour you a glass, then?

He turns the corkscrew too quickly and pierces the bottom of the cork. I see some pieces fall into the wine. I hold back a grimace, but my shudder doesn't escape him. He gives me the side-eye, expecting my usual *smooth move,* or better yet, my oh-so-friendly *now you've ruined it,* or that old standby *oh, great!* He's heard me say these things to Alice before, when scolding her for this kind of slip-up.

I say nothing.

He pours me some; little bits of cork float on the surface of my glass.

I take a mouthful. *It's good, thanks.*

While I peel potatoes, he settles into his chair with his feet up, arms crossed. He slurps his wine loudly.

You doing that on purpose?

I'm criticizing him outright. Must be having trouble controlling myself tonight.

It's a wine-tasting thing.

I put the pan down on the hot pad and sit down across from him. He looks at his glass, his plate, my forehead, his plate, his glass.

I have an interview tomorrow.

That was a huge bite of steak. I'll chew it slowly before answering, so I don't seem overly interested. It'll be perfect.

Where at?

In Montréal. A waste management position with the City.

I thought he'd stay the year. That he'd look for a job in the area. What's he doing exactly, sending CVs to the other side of the planet?

Cool.

Yup, I said it, I said "cool." My vocabulary is equal to my wit.

Silence except for more or less subtle chewing sounds as we eat.

My plate finally empty, I grab the bottle to pour the last drops into my goblet. He looks at me with almost total indifference.

So, what's it like, sleeping with a guy?

I choke on my mouthful of wine; he smiles.

That's what I thought.

what he heard

Eloy's room.

Eloy sits at the desk with his back to the door, playing a video game.

Alice comes in and sits on his bed.

ALICE
> I came to invade your space.

ELOY
> Make yourself at home.

Silence.

Eloy keeps playing.

ALICE
> I needed to get out a bit.

ELOY
> You're still inside.

ALICE
> You know what I mean.

ELOY
> If only you always said what you mean.

Alice sighs.

Silence.

ALICE
> Comfy mattress.

Silence.

ALICE
> What're you doing?

ELOY
> Nothing much.

ALICE
> Still. You *are* doing *something.*

ELOY
> Not really.

Alice lies down on his bed and taps away at her cell phone.

ALICE
> Am I bothering you?

ELOY
> Nope.

ALICE
> You sure?

ELOY
> Yup.

ALICE
> And what about you, do *you* always say what you mean?

ELOY
Nope.

Silence.

ALICE
You're unpleasant.

ELOY
One of my best qualities.

Silence.

ALICE
Why don't you open the curtains?

ELOY
Causes screen glare.

Alice drops her cell phone. It lands on her face. She gives a little shout of surprise.

Eloy doesn't look up.

Alice puts the phone in her pocket. She coughs a little.

ALICE
Actually, I wanted to talk to you about something.

ELOY
Shoot.

ALICE *ignores the double meaning*
Something that makes me uncomfortable.

ELOY
Okay...?

ALICE

> See, around here, we try to share what's on our minds as
> soon as it comes up.

ELOY

> Okay...

ALICE

> And I've slept in the girls' room for a few nights in a row
> over the last while.

ELOY

> Mm hmm.

ALICE

> And I was wondering.

Silence.

ALICE

> Do you hear us?

ELOY

> I generally do, if you talk to me.

Alice sighs.

ALICE

> You know very well what I mean.

ELOY

> It would help if you said what you meant.

ALICE

> Oh, for fuck sakes!

Eloy keeps looking at the screen.

ALICE *exasperated*
>
> When Camille, Gayle and I are fucking, can you hear us?

ELOY *mockingly*
>
> Ohhh!

Alice sighs again. Eloy pauses his game and turns to face her.

ELOY
>
> What does it matter if I can hear you or not?

ALICE
>
> I dunno. I just want to know so I can, you know, *adjust.*

ELOY
>
> You don't have to *adjust* anything on my account.

ALICE
>
> Still. I would like to know.

ELOY
>
> Honestly, I don't give a shit.

ALICE
>
> So, you *can* hear us.

ELOY
>
> I didn't say that.

ALICE
>
> Eloy!

ELOY
>
> What?

ALICE
>
> Can you hear us, or can't you?

Eloy sighs.

Silence. Alice waits solemnly, eyebrow raised.

ELOY
>Yes, I can hear you.

Alice presses her lips together.

ALICE
>Okay.

ELOY
>I couldn't care less. Really.

ALICE
>Maybe not, but *I* do.

ELOY
>Why?

ALICE
>Because.

ELOY
>You're pretty cryptic today.

ALICE
>Because it's private, what we do together, okay?

ELOY
>I've seen you naked, you know.

ALICE
>Ten years ago.

ELOY

> You haven't changed much. I see you braless in the morn-
> ing, don't forget.

ALICE

> So classy.

ELOY

> Not bad, by the way.

Silence.

Eloy goes back to his game.

ALICE

> So, let's say we fuck tonight...

ELOY

> You and me?

ALICE, *resigned*

> Whatever, if you want.

ELOY

> Don't tempt me.

ALICE

> I meant me and those two.

ELOY

> Yeah?

ALICE

> Could you tell me in the morning if you heard anything?

ELOY

> Why?

ALICE

> Because I'm asking you to. Like I said, it makes me uncomfortable.

ELOY

> I'm not sure.

ALICE

> Please?

ELOY

> I don't want to indulge your sexual hang-ups.

Silence.

ALICE

> I can't believe I have to beg.

ELOY

> I'm not hating it.

ALICE *both discouraged and disgusted*

> Ew.

ELOY

> I can sleep in the living room. Or put on headphones. Or tell you to fuck louder so I can hear better.

ALICE *gets up and heads for the door*

> Fuck off.

ELOY

> Okay, okay, sorry, okay! Seriously, I'm not losing sleep over it!

ALICE

> Forget it.

ELOY

> Aw, my Li-la...

Alice pauses in the doorway.

ELOY

> Come back, sit down.

ALICE

> You're such a pain.

ELOY

> You love me anyway.

ALICE

> "Love" is a strong word.

She sits on the end of the bed.

ELOY

> While we're at it, I wanted to ask you something.

Silence.

ELOY

> About Simon.

ALICE

> Oh boy.

ELOY

> I get the feeling he's looking at me.

ALICE
>It's unavoidable.

ELOY
>He looks at me a lot.

ALICE
>And?

ELOY
>Is it supposed to mean something?

ALICE
>Gayle must look at you just as much, but you're oblivious.

Eloy stares at her in disbelief.

ALICE *goes up to him, puts her hand on his shoulder*
>You're easy on the eyes, tiger. That's all it means.

Silence. They look at each other.

ALICE
>Does it bug you?

ELOY
>No, it's not that.

ALICE
>You can tell him to stop, you know.

ELOY
>It isn't that.

ALICE
>Then what?

ELOY

It's just...strange.

ALICE

Why?

ELOY

I'm not used to it.

ALICE

Used to what?

ELOY

Getting checked out by a guy.

camille

making yet another ham quiche

I bought frozen, ready-to-bake pie shells. Tenderflake.

Fuck, I hate Wednesdays. Who made up the schedule? I can't remember anymore. A spreadsheet tells us who cooks which meal on which day. Alice might have given us the impression we were coming up with it together, but I think she already had it all done up and asked us *does this work for you?* so we could approve it quickly and get back to pounding nails, keyboards, or butts. She's Machiavellian like that.

Kitchens aren't my kind of place. I'm a back-alley girl, a treetop girl, a crazy-carpeting-down-snowy-slopes girl. *A bedroom girl* Gayle would say, rewarding me with an elbow to the ribs. Always so classy, my sweetheart.

It's already 5:30 when I get home. I took my time at the store. Maybe it's the change of hormone dosage but I found the little orange-themed Halloween cupcakes particularly moving. They reminded me of the Pillsbury Slice 'n Bake cookies my dad used to make when I was little, the ones with the pumpkin design in the middle, and my nostalgia surprised me, I never think of him anymore. When I open the door on the fifth, I find Eloy and Simon sitting on either end of the kitchen table, eyes riveted to their respective computers. I take off my boots, my raincoat, my nice hat. I say *hello kids!* and no reaction, not even a lifted eyebrow or a nod of the head.

Gayle, now *she* heard me. She comes out of our room—usually she's in the living room, so she must have wanted to give them their *privacy*—and gives me a kiss. Out of the corner of my eye, I see Eloy lift his head a touch.

Maude brought us another box of clothes! All excited, my love leads me into the living room to show me the extent of new wardrobe possibilities. *There's some really nice pieces but some horror shows, too.* So I'm not the only one who's fashion challenged. That's reassuring. *It's old stuff from high school!* Maude apparently protested—as though that were any excuse. Me, I might as well be fifteen, although I do look old for a teenager. I'm just starting to get hips, I barely fill an A cup, and have at least a year of these "changes" to go. I have no idea what looks good on me.

Oh actually, that's not true! I do know one thing looks good: form-fitting Lycra boxers. I made Eloy blush this morning when I came out of my room in my "pyjamas" and bent over to pet the big cat.

Alice, Gayle and I crowd around the big box of clothes in the living room, while our non-skirt-wearing roommates steal glances. We spend about an hour trying on Maude's old clothes, until Eloy addresses the whole peanut gallery—*When are we eating?*—at the precise moment Alice is inquiring as to the effect a bra has on her chest—*I would never pay full price for a padded bra like this.* I grumblingly put back on the hideous clothes I've worn all day and get down to cutting up broccoli at the kitchen counter.

Quiche is what I make when I don't feel like making anything, which is to say at least every other week. The others can't take any more quiche, I know this, it makes me laugh. If only they had the guts to tell me to stop making it, but it will never happen, they're too polite.

The girls get dressed and come to sit at the table to keep me company and bug the two cuties who have stayed in the kitchen. I'm still amazed this is working—five of us, *we five*, together. Simon has stopped bitching about Eloy behind his back. Eloy has started letting Gayle pet the cat when he's holding it—huge progress. Even our official stress cadet Alice has stopped asking us not-so-subtly, multiple times a day, if everything's okay, if we need anything, if this or that person is bothering us, if she can help us in any way—basically *are you all happy and if you're not, is it my fault?* She may prefer being the one tied to the bed, but she loses her shit if she's not the one in control.

Speaking of Alice, irked by my laziness, she's taken the knife out of my hands and is taking care of the vegetables and ham. *Start grating the cheese, or we'll be here till midnight.*

I'm almost comfortable with Eloy now. When I started wearing skirts around him, he didn't say a word. He never misgenders me. He pays his rent every month, on time.

That said, I'm still waiting for Alice to stop giving him the special attention paid a new arrival. What's worse, she's not the only one. Simon pays him just as much attention—in a passive-aggressive way, but still. She's the angel and he's the stuck-up bitch. Even my own sweetheart Gayle sucks up to him because he's amusing. You'd think she'd adopted a new pet.

And now Alice has taken over making dinner even though it's not her turn but, oh well, she doesn't seem to mind. *Pour the eggs, honey, the oven is preheated.*

Eloy and I have no interest in each other. I'm not sure how to handle it. It's so rare for me to leave people cold, even when I ignore them. I'd rather be fantasizing about him too, swooning when he gets out of the shower, melting when he smiles, batting my eyelashes hard enough to set off a tornado in Texas.

But I don't feel a thing. Cold as the first spring dip in Lake Magog.

No, I don't share the Family's excitement over the new recruit. In fact, I feel like I no longer have anything in common with these people, crowding around him while I keep my distance. I'm the only one who has no interest in getting close to him. And yet I don't ask for much, only to be granted some time, to be given commands—kneel, don't move, present yourself for fingering, permission to come in 5, 4, 3...In exchange, I offer my profuse gratitude. That and one hell of a good tongue job, if desired.

Would you get over this dude already? Go play with yourselves while you look at his picture, why don't you? Maybe that'll take the edge off.

Great, now I've overcooked it and burned the cheese. Sigh. We sit at the table regardless. It's quite edible, as it turns out.

Deflated, Eloy plays with his food.

Quiche again?

The others stare at him, stunned. I wait for them to come to my defence. No one sticks their neck out. I want to yank his plate away and mash the quiche into his face. It's just a touch trashier than a cream pie.

alice

furiously blending butternut squash soup

Whenever I purée soup with the hand blender, Camille stands behind me snickering. Every time.

I should remind her how immature she is. It's just a plain old up-and-down motion. What's so dirty about it? *Go on, get behind me to show me how it's done, then you'll see.*

But not in front of Eloy, please, it makes me uncomfortable. I'm baffled. Stop.

Just because we were together once, he and I, doesn't mean it's comfortable. We were sixteen, living with our parents, and I've forgotten the details, you know? I forget whether he likes spicy food and toss practically a whole jar of cayenne into the soup.

Camille's a sweetheart, she'll understand. If I say stop it, she will. She doesn't know yet—I haven't been able to tell her because *shame*—but he's the reason that for a long time I thought I wasn't good enough. If I forget for one second that I'm not sixteen anymore, that my body's my own and I have a right to take up space, Eloy the Teenager comes back to me, condescending and judgmental. I remember so clearly him mocking me if I got distracted and absent-mindedly gave a simple answer to a question requiring more than a "yes." How he would go so far as to say *should I draw you a picture?* Or if

I was, say, grilling hot dog buns and burned them: *Too hard a job for you, eh?* Or even worse, if I pulled an all-nighter to finish my homework: *Guess you shouldn't have wasted time all week chatting till 3 a.m.* So now, if he says so much as, "could you...," I hear *you're a piece of shit.* It's like when someone invites me to go for a run and all I hear is my dad making fun of me, then ditching me; *If you ran any slower, you'd be backing up.* A memory that gives me the immediate and overwhelming urge to sob.

Even though I know intellectually he's changed, that he's a different person, more than a decade later, my body still doesn't. It still goes into panic mode without warning. The only thing my body remembers of those eight months with Eloy is being accused of being *too complicated*: if having his dick inside me didn't make me come; if having his fingers on my clit didn't make me come; if having his tongue between my legs didn't make me come, it was *my* mechanics that needed fixing. Sheepishly, I would play the *never-mind-it-still-feels-good-I'm-into-it* card. And it was true: I was grateful for his desire, for the *sacrifice* he was making, putting up with me, me and my defective body.

If he tried too hard, I'd get anxious, which would just make it worse.

Pretty soon Camille is going to start bugging me to chuckle over all of her hand-job jokes again. I'll lose my patience and be forced (!) to go sulk in my room. As if that will make a difference. As if it will stop her from accusing me of not having a sense of humour.

He's not here, you know.

I'm still hovering over the pot when Gayle wraps her arms around me, clasping her hands together over my belly.

I exhale stiffly, like I'm breathing through a pressurized tube. The heat of her body against my back softens me instantly and I start trembling. The soup is silky smooth and here I am, still blending away like a madwoman. Wonder how she knew what was bothering me.

Go sit down. How about I set the table? Everything's ready, right? Let me take care of the rest. You seem tired.

I don't look in the mirror very much, my Sorceress of Love, I don't know how I look; but I *am* tired, tired from spending too much energy being curious and terrified all at once. I can't seem to *move on.* I have to satisfy my appetite somehow, although maybe what I want is not *him* exactly but *knowledge.* I want to know if his cock, his fingers, his tongue would make me come now. Now that he must have learned more attentiveness and dexterity through experience with others. I wonder if he would say *your pussy scared me back then*—the only excuse that makes sense, that would explain why he didn't explore it completely. Why else wouldn't he? Isn't that what you do when you visit someplace new?

The Family knows I'm tired, that I'll leave them be, but if I stop talking, if I don't help Gayle fill the silence while we all inhale our soup, who else will?

If he could hear me right now, he would probably say his youthful neglect was just as much my fault as his, that I didn't speak up about what was bothering me so he had no reason to doubt me when I said *it's okay.* And he'd have a point. Teenage me wasn't exactly up-front. And I would say *oh, shut your mouth.* I'm not rehashing the past so you can defend yourself. I just want to stop obsessing about how it shaped me, defined me, influenced me, deformed me.

I'm still staring into the soup when I finally decide to say something.

Is it okay to accuse him of having damaged me?

Gayle squeezes me harder.

Simon looks at me with disdain, brow furrowed.

Why do you do that?

Do what?

Give him so much importance.

dark mornings

(january)

camille

1 a.m.

I don't know if she's trying to make him jealous, but it's working.

No, she wouldn't do that on purpose. Alice won't stand for the idea of jealousy being a measure of someone's affection. *I love therefore I get jealous*: no way.

All the same. He didn't expect it and was surprised.

I'm saying this as though it didn't affect me: that's a ploy. As the bottom, the one who chooses to submit, I always consider myself the strongest, but sometimes I flinch. I handle unexpected blows remarkably well, but this took us all by surprise. She hasn't ever brought anyone home yet, not since we've lived here.

Me, I'm not jealous of anyone. I manage information. I just manage it less well when new information emerges unexpectedly, that's all.

As she was leaving, she said *not sure I'll be home after*. She finds a show to go to every week—she's too sociable, really, you have to ask yourself what we have in common—and she comes home at an ungodly hour, but she usually does come home. That she bothered to warn us she might not come home implied she would run into Benjamin, and it goes without saying that running into Benjamin ends with a sleepover.

Benjamin. Not his real name, FYI. At dinner one night,

I said he reminded me of a turtle. Don't get the wrong idea. He's a pretty handsome guy, my kind of dude, with long arms, square shoulders, a hint of beard showcasing plump lips— *plump and soft,* according to Alice's detailed description. But anyway, a turtle, because he hunches his shoulders so much, it looks like he wants to crawl into himself. *Benjamin the turtle.* The name stuck.

Benjamin, Alice's only lover. He never sleeps here, she goes to his place every so often, it's not even a monthly thing. Just a lover with soft lips.

It's 12:30 a.m. Simon, Eloy and I are in the living room with our laptops for our usual *Diablo* mission to wrap up the night. I play—yes, you guessed it, a barbarian. It doesn't make me any less of a lady.

So when Simon and Eloy sat beside each other on the couch (for the first time ever!), I couldn't comment on it to anyone and was miffed: this sudden closeness was quite the event, considering their spats on the daily.

I'm not expecting Alice home, so when I hear the door open at 12:45, I nearly blurt out *Alice, you gotta see this! They're cruising each other* right out in the open*!* Then I hear a laugh. Laughs, plural.

Stunned, the guys look up toward the front door at the same time as me, abandoning our characters. The sound of them dying horrible deaths intensifies, then abruptly stops.

The duo reaches the space between the kitchen and living room. Benjamin still has his coat on—the coat hooks are overflowing and well, the ambient temperature is around sixteen degrees in the house, so wearing a coat makes sense. Meanwhile, we have blankets over our shoulders and computers to warm our laps...In short, having his coat on inside doesn't seem all that strange.

Alice whispers to him *first door on the right.* He slips away to hide and without giving us a second glance, closes the door very quietly (you gotta appreciate that). He might take his coat off before getting under the covers, but I doubt it; it's the coldest room in the house, complete with defective radiator.

She's clearly drunk. She grins a devilish grin, one that says *so sorry, I couldn't help it.*

Girls will be girls and all that crap.

She comes over and murmurs *good night,* bends to kiss me and then Simon. That's when she finally notices he and Eloy are sitting on the same couch. Her eyes go wide, telling Eloy with those magnificent wild eyes of hers that she can't believe it but is very pleased. Him, she doesn't kiss.

She takes a step back, smiles even bigger and says *I'll spare you.*

He says *why?* probably thinking she'll catch the irony in his voice. But she doesn't even hesitate, she kisses him square on the lips for five Mississippis before turning away and going to join the turtle in her room.

Eloy looks at Simon, Simon looks at Eloy. I look at them looking at each other.

Simon closes the lid of his computer, thumps off to his room and slams the door.

Eloy mumbles *fuck* and drags himself off to his room as well, but leaves his door ajar, as usual. For the cats.

I get up and claim the abandoned couch. I stretch all the way out and play *Diablo* by myself until 3 a.m.

gayle

4 a.m.

I wake up thirsty. Reaching out to grab my water bottle, I knock my glasses off and accidentally turn on the radio, which gets the cats yowling at the door. All I want is a drink. I mash my lips onto the spout of the Nalgene but, apparently, I'm not lined up, I'm slightly off the mark so the wannabe gulp of water pours right between my breasts, where my skin is the most delicate, and pools in the middle part of my bra. Lake Cleavage.

It's cold and it pisses me off and I hate being wet.

I use the sheet to dry myself off. Now I'm stuck with a soaked sheet. Fuck. Might as well get up now.

It's still dark—no, it's the colour of streetlights-on-fresh-snow. Wow, I'm inspired, even at this hour. I should get a job at Benjamin Moore.

Even after the commotion with the radio, Camille hasn't budged, and when I get out of bed, she grunts something—not talking to me, I don't think. I quickly assess the pros and cons of putting on a robe before leaving the room. After all, I'm in my underwear and Eloy is so easily traumatized, I wouldn't want to break him.

But I love the shiver of cold air on my skin. Fuck the robe.

I open the door a crack, check right, check left, and slip to the bathroom with the cats following behind.

The light over the sink stings my eyes and annoys the big cat, who starts caterwauling like a queen in heat. *Shhh* I plead; he just gives me a confused look with his tongue sticking out. So rude.

The mirror shows me what I'd hoped: a clump of hair poised acrobatically atop my head, a feat accomplished by hitting the pillow with my hair still wet from the shower. Perfect. The cat scrolls and unscrolls around my calves, still meowling away. I use a yellowing washcloth to clean off the smudged eyeliner from my bad removal job last night.

I give my bush a scratch. The hair on my outer lips makes a raspy sound: there's a textural logic to it. My nails get into it—it feels good, what can I say—and in their fervour wind up venturing into the folds in question. Huh. Still wet. I grab some toilet paper to dry myself, and before there's even time to realize my discharge is strangely clumpy, I'm furiously scratching my vulva.

Fuck me.

Yeast infection.

My family doctor recently recommended I "reduce the frequency of sexual encounters" because it could be a contributing cause of my frequent vaginal infections. My poor "hypersensitive" pussy doesn't want me having so much fun.

And yet I'm not delicate. I have big bones with lots of meat on them. It runs in the family, even though my mother and sisters wage a fierce battle against our blubbery genes. I have big pores and hairy limbs. I have dark, thick hair everywhere actually, around my nipples and on my chin. Hairs so wiry, I could use them for toothpicks.

I'm not delicate. My palms are bone dry. The lines on them are so defined, a blind fortune teller could read them. I could cut steak with my toenail. My eyebrows are dark forests that would make great camping spots.

My body runs well. It's efficient and devoted to my well-being, for the most part. There was a time when these little chats with my body weren't so cool, leading to some sketchy sugar-free diets, but it should be noted that the conversation between me, my body and my mother has always been defective. Since I blocked one of those communication channels (my mother, my body) things are going much better. Still, my body rebels against my seemingly insatiable desire.

My desire is an issue. It increases over time and that alone makes getting older a wonderful thing. I masturbate daily but that doesn't mean I'm obsessed. I love both women and men but that doesn't mean I'm confused. The effect a whip has on a willing back drives me wild, but that doesn't mean I'm crazy any more than disliking penetration makes me an untouchable saint. Demanding respect from my colleagues doesn't mean I'm pretentious and not speaking to my parents anymore doesn't mean I'm ungrateful. I'm not a coward for saying "no" to things I don't want. Requiring consent before being touched doesn't mean I'm stubborn and falling in love with someone else's partner doesn't make me a homewrecker. I'm neither too sensitive, nor too complex, nor too intense. I'm neither too gorgeous nor very ugly, neither too open nor too closed-off.

Fifteen-year-old Gayle would tell thirty-year-old me: *You love yourself too much.* Thirty-year-old Gayle would tell fifteen-year-old Gayle: *Shut yer pie-hole.*

If only my vagina loved me as much as I love my vagina.

The big cat chimes in with meows. *Okay, okay, I'll feed you.* I'm leaving the bathroom, with my hand still on my crotch and my head down, trying to avoid the felines as I go, when I run

into a human-shaped obstacle, most likely waiting for me to
vacate the bathroom.

I can't see his face with my nose buried in his chest, but I
can tell from the scent it isn't one of the Family.

Benjamin, what the fuck are you doing lurking out here?

Okay, no, I don't say that, I don't say anything, I just think
it. I raise my head and give him a look. The glaring kind.

Not perturbed in the least, this one. He gently takes me by
the shoulders and unglues me from his chest, steps aside, goes
into the bathroom and shuts the door.

eloy

8 a.m.

I waited for him to be gone before leaving my room. I heard the sound of goodbyes, wet smooching, the front door opening and closing, footsteps echoing along the hall and down the stairs. A few minutes later, I opened my door.

Now she's sitting at the table with her Ministry of Magic mug, holding a thick novel open behind her half-bagel.

The floor creaks under my bare feet. She looks up and whispers *Good morning.*

Not really, no. My ears and I are worn out from a night spent mostly listening for sounds, the ones that would inevitably come from her room. But precisely because she was in *her* room, the one furthest away of all, I didn't hear a thing.

To be honest, for two hours I had the impression all of us were stock still in our rooms, pressing our (unperturbed, embarrassed, or plugged) ears to our respective walls, eavesdropping on the two of them. I fell asleep when I heard Camille go to bed—probably the only sound I managed to discern. I wasn't upset about not hearing anything, I just realized it has become a regular part of my nightly routine: leave the door open so the cats can come in and out, then get undressed in the dark, slide under the quilt, and fall asleep to the sound of spankings.

There's coffee is what she says, quietly, while picking up the chunk of bagel.

Yay.

I head over to the coffee machine, noticing I'm slightly queasy. Probably not a good idea to have coffee.

(You say that like it's going to stop you.)

I notice Gayle's long body sprawled out on the couch, wrapped in her Snuggie: that explains why Alice is whispering. And yet, Gayle was in bed by ten last night.

(Don't try to understand it.)

Did you sleep well?

I never sleep well, she knows that, but she asks me every morning anyways, without exception. And I always answer "meh."

Meh.

I join her at the table. I try to cup the mug in both hands but it burns my palms. The handle is too small. I blow on it— the coffee, not the handle.

I'm sorry about yesterday.

Is she apologizing for kissing me or for bringing an interloper home? Which situation led to me sleeping badly?

You were drunk.

That's no excuse.

Well, still.

Maybe I'm being too nice, excusing her, but it's not like I hated it.

You were sitting beside Simon.

So?

I'm using one of them (her, not him) to get closer to the other (to him, not her), at least a little bit, and I've been found out (by her, not him). I'm confused about him. I'm just barely admitting it to myself, but saying it out loud? Double "meh."

What does she see in him, I want to ask.

Every day, I put up with him crashing about. I hear him washing vigorously, watch him fastidiously tidy stuff up even if it isn't his. His strident laughter makes me grit my teeth. I catch him going through the motions of getting dressed, stare at him obsessively drying the countertop. Every day I wind up in front of his alphabetized bookshelf. The living room blinds lowered to exactly mid-window. The perfectly coiled up vacuum cleaner hose.

He gets on my nerves.

When Gayle and I were both home for lunch once, she took the opportunity to explain how Simon is a *tsundere*, a portmanteau of the Japanese "tsuntsun"—*arrogant and unpleasant on first acquaintance*—and "deredere"—*very endearing once you manage to get close.*

I didn't ask for all this attention. It's a drag. *I don't know what I'm doing and I'm not sure I care.* Not that I said it out loud.

Alice goes back to her novel; I stare at the wall. One of the cats—the big one—climbs onto my lap. Gayle, still stretched out on the couch, makes a lustful humming sound.

Anyway, it's not like you were noisy.

She looks at me again, her forehead creased.

I hear you with the girls, but I didn't hear you with him.

And?

It was weird. I'm used to it by now.

She narrows her eyes and probes me as she so loves to do.

I don't get you.

There's nothing to get, that's what's so funny.

alice

<u>8:15 a.m.</u>

It's done. I did the test and aced it. I'd rather change course, though. This one doesn't work for me at all. Sleeping with him at his place is way better than bringing him back here.

Besides, last month when I was leaving his place at three in the morning, I had an epiphany: my car is as good for getting home in the middle of the night after a booty-call as it is for getting to it in the first place. Back in the day, a woman who wanted to visit her lover and didn't have a car was obliged to wait, to play the dependent role while at the mercy of his desires and schedule. And even if he lived close enough for her to get home on foot, how many women would risk walking alone in the middle of the night, even if just for a kilometre?

My car and my unpredictable libido go well together.

I like Benjamin, but not enough to invite him to stay the night again. I wanted to kick him out after the third quasi-satisfying fuck, but he was already asleep. It probably traumatized the peeps, but at least I tested it out once. Just to see.

I kind of would've liked to have breakfast alone. But if I'd gone to eat in my room, Gayle would've come to ask if everything was okay, or Simon would have come purring, wanting to cuddle.

Even though I just apologized to Eloy for kissing him,

it still feels weird. I have the urge to touch him, but I'm uncomfortable. If I reach out with my foot, I could touch his calf. Maybe his knee. His thighs—just the tops of them, okay, maybe *between* them if I was a little crazy.

I could say *my legs are sore, do you mind if I stretch them out?* And just rest them there, on his chair, between his legs.

It's hard for me not to touch all the time. It's my thing.

Once upon a time, I *could* touch Eloy, which only makes this worse. Now, when I move closer, he pulls away.

I often wonder how Emily managed to get close to him in this era of instant messaging. For me, there was no trying to figure out if he was into me by looking for signs. There was no *did his calf just touch mine on purpose?* at the movies. No *does he ask his other female friends out for a beer on a Saturday?*

Nope. Instead, for sixteen-year-old me, it was straight to "I love you" via email. To draw out the anticipation, I sent it right before I left for Maine with my parents. I timed it to draw out the suspense. I left the possibility of there being a "me too" waiting for me out in the Interweb hanging for two weeks.

I was in love with someone I'd never seen. My body wasn't part of that love, but that changed fast, so fast once I finally met him. Once I touched him. Kissed and caressed him. Fucked him. I couldn't let it go and oh, how I talked and talked about it! So much that my "friends" treated me like a sex maniac.

(Oh, high school, what do you know of desire?)

Looking back, I knew what I was feeling was love because I trusted my body. The most important rule was: *Lose your virginity with someone you love.* Which begged the question: *How do you know you're in love?* And the standard response was, as always: *When it happens, you'll just know!* When it finally happens, you feel the world come tumbling down in your belly and you tell yourself *now I know what they're talking about!* But it isn't *you* who knows. It's your body.

The body knows it way more than you do.

Sometimes your body knows it even if the object of your desire is a fucking loser. What no one ever tells you—what they forget to mention—is that you can also listen to your head.

Because honestly, that feeling in your gut? It's not exactly the epitome of wisdom.

Same with jealousy. Your body doesn't consult you when it senses a threat. If it senses someone is about to replace you, you'll be forced to puke your guts out before letting you give up.

But what does your body know, exactly? That you're scared? So what else is new?

My body also has memories, as if I needed more of them. Yesterday, fifteen years after our first fuck, my lips on Eloy's still felt the same. My hand on his cheek felt the same. His oily hair brushing the tips of my fingers felt the same.

And after that, I went back to rubbing up against Benjamin. It wasn't the same.

Eloy?

He sips his coffee very, very loudly while looking up at me—either to get a rise out of me or make me laugh, or both.

I'd like to kiss you again.

He sets his cup down, stares into it. From where I'm sitting, I can't tell if there's still coffee in it.

My stomach aches.

I don't think that's a good idea.

simon

8:30 a.m.

I just want some coffee. Carry on, by all means. Don't mind me.

I had to do something. I didn't overhear anything; one glance was all it took and I knew: these two are about to French in front of everyone.

Storming into the kitchen and using my most passive-aggressive tone was clearly the solution.

I go to the cupboard, open it, grab a mug, close the door a little too quickly, a little too hard, the mugs rattle on the shelf. The one I'm holding in my hand might as well be a brass knuckle, I'm gripping it so tightly. I should pour the coffee in over the sink, my hands are shaking a bit.

The poor things have stopped talking, probably sensing my oppressive vibe.

My feet stick to the polished tiles as I walk over to the fridge to get the milk. I can feel the weight of their gazes and barely manage to stop myself from walking more loudly. Let them put up with my presence, may I ram it down their throats—they seem to like that kind of thing.

Camille comes out of her room looking like someone died. It wasn't *her* I meant to disturb—collateral damage.

Gayle?

Gayle raises her head—what's she doing sleeping on the couch?—and smiles at her lover who joins her and covers her face with loud sloppy kisses.

I sit at the head of the table, one lover on either side of me, with my back to Gayle and Camille; I can still hear them kissing anyway.

Alice leans toward me.

Honey, could you please calm down? Benjamin is gone.

Whatever. Benjamin, that lunatic. He doesn't bother me one bit. He doesn't even have a degree.

Somehow, I can tell this isn't the first time they're having breakfast together, but usually I'm gone, already out the door before the Others even drag themselves as far as the shower.

It's obscene. Putting themselves on display like that, obnoxiously parading their love as if the whole place belonged to them, as if no one were forced to put up with it.

I'm not talking about the women necking behind me.

I want a bowl of cereal, the Special K on the bottom shelf, the one no one eats because when it comes to pantries, you only eat what's right in front of you. But if I get up for a) the cereal and b) the milk, I'll wind up with my back to them and lose whatever control I regained by sitting between them.

I have a moral obligation to keep tabs on them.

Alice is still looking at me. I haven't responded to her remark about her undergraduate lover.

She touches my shoulder, pats it a little. In other words, an incredibly condescending *there, there.*

I wrap my fingers around her wrist, lift her hand off me and put it back on the table.

She adds: *The others never made you act like this. What's the problem?*

She doesn't get it, poor thing. The lovebirds on the couch are watching us now, judging my behaviour impolite, shitty even. Even Eloy gets that he's the problem. He leans back in his chair—aw, do you feel bad, my dearest? So much the better. It's what you deserve.

I take a big gulp of coffee. I have nothing to say to him.

I'm not sure what's he's thinking, touching my calf with his bare foot at this precise moment, when my mouth is still full. Wasn't that time with the wine enough to satisfy his desire to humiliate me? I don't choke this time, thankfully. I just bang my knee against the underside of the table. Eloy is stone-faced as always. It's just Alice looking at me right now, as though I were completely disturbed—disturbed as in insane, not as in bothered because it's obvious I am bothered—wondering if I've lost it.

He touched me. Was it an accident, or is he trying to tell me something? I don't know him well enough to figure it out. I can't read him very well. Me, I don't analyze people as though they were literary characters. If I ask Alice—*He touched me, what does that mean?*—she might help, but then she'd know that I'm attempting to analyze and therefore that I notice what he does, and therefore that what he does interests me.

My hands are visibly shaking despite my commanding them to stop. His cold toes press against me again, firmly, this time on my foot. He leaves them there, so I get that he's doing it deliberately, but that doesn't explain why. He slurps the last of his coffee, Alice gives him a scolding look, as though the annoying sound might provoke me into flipping the table.

Not that we'd lose much; the plates are already empty and this dish set is hideous.

I didn't hear Camille getting up, yet suddenly her lips are glued to my left ear and her too-long nails are drumming the back of my chair.

C'mon babe, let's make a little visit to my room.

what she thought best to remind him

Camille and Gayle's room.

Enter Camille (forest-green fleece robe), steering Simon (light-blue cotton t-shirt and grey flannel bottoms) into the room.

He drags himself over to the two desks at the back of the room. He plunks down into one of the office chairs, grabs hold of the armrests, closes his eyes and takes a deep breath.

Camille sits in the other chair and swivels around while looking up at the ceiling.

CAMILLE *sighs, resigned*
> Talk to me.

SIMON *being coy*
> Whatever.

Camille stops swivelling, lifts her feet up onto the chair and hugs her knees.

CAMILLE *resting her head on her knees*
> We can play guessing games all day if you like.

SIMON

Don't feel like talking about it.

CAMILLE

Me neither. That works out well, eh?

Simon sighs.

CAMILLE

C'mon, out with it. I didn't drag you outta there for nothing.

SIMON

You shouldn't have.

CAMILLE

You were about to torch the tablecloth. I love that tablecloth.

SIMON

You can't let those two out of your sight for a second.

CAMILLE

They're adults, you know. All grown up and everything.

SIMON

Can't be trusted.

CAMILLE

Who, Alice?

SIMON

Oh, come on! I mean Eloy.

CAMILLE

Is it supposed to be obvious who you mean?

SIMON

It *is* obvious.

CAMILLE

Okay, so tell me, why can't he be trusted?

SIMON

He's hurt her before.

CAMILLE

She left *him*, right?

SIMON

And how come, do you think?

CAMILLE

I never asked her. Did she tell you?

SIMON

No. But why else would she leave?

CAMILLE

She's the one who offered *him* a place here.

SIMON

Maybe she has an incurable case of Stockholm Syndrome, how should I know?

CAMILLE *blinks slowly*

You're not making any sense right now.

SIMON

What do you mean?

CAMILLE

> Well, did she leave *you* because you did something to hurt her?

SIMON

> That's different.

CAMILLE

> Oh right, this is different, because you're so special.

SIMON

> You don't get it.

CAMILLE

> So, explain it to me then, just for fun.

Silence.

Simon fumes with his eyes closed for a long while.

Camille spins around in her chair until he starts talking again.

SIMON *quietly, almost whispering*

> It's just that...he's like me. Only...*better.*

CAMILLE

> Only what?

SIMON

> Better!

CAMILLE

> Better how?

SIMON

> He's more...in shape, let's say.

CAMILLE *mockingly*

> Ha!

SIMON *sheepishly*

> What? It's true!

CAMILLE

> Even if it is, I don't see how that makes him better.

SIMON

> Well, it can't hurt, that's for sure.

CAMILLE

> Nonsense, you're making a big issue out of nothing.

Silence.

CAMILLE

> You'll need to explain what his god-like physique has to do with you being "uneasy."

SIMON

> If he's better than me, and she can have him, why would she still want me?

CAMILLE

> He's not better than you. He's just another dude.

SIMON

> That doesn't help, if you know what I mean.

CAMILLE

> No, I don't know what you mean. At all.

SIMON

> It's not my fault you don't get it.

CAMILLE

No, I don't get it. Do you hear yourself right now? What, are you twelve all of a sudden? Are you telling me you feel threatened because Eloy's a *guy*?

Silence. Simon stares at the floor.

SIMON

A little.

CAMILLE *rolling her eyes*

Aye yai yai.

SIMON

You really don't see how that matters, eh?

CAMILLE

I don't, no.

Camille's attitude and body language slowly shifts from "sad and serious" to "tense and stressed." She seems to want to move away from Simon.

SIMON

The guys she sleeps with are just friends, usually. Since we got back together, she's only had female lovers. But this guy...she's getting attached to.

CAMILLE

So? What does that change?

Simon shrugs.

CAMILLE

I'll tell you what that changes. Absolutely nothing, Simon.

SIMON

I'm uncomfortable.

CAMILLE *propels herself backwards, arms raised as though shouting "Eureka!"*

Finally! So this is about *you*, not Alice. She's got nothing to do with it.

SIMON

Alice has everything to do with it.

CAMILLE

You and Eloy are two different people.

SIMON

I need her.

CAMILLE

I do too. So?

SIMON

He'll wind up replacing me.

Camille shakes her head.

CAMILLE

Aye yai yai.

SIMON

Quit saying that. You have no idea what it's like.

CAMILLE

Oh, but I do, I know very fucking well, in fact.

SIMON

Oh yeah?

CAMILLE

Yeah, because even if she loves him—don't look at me like that, of course she loves him, we all know that except him—even if she loves him and it hurts the Big Man's poor little ego, this is what you wanted, isn't it, my dear? To accept that you can't be everything to her because trying to be already destroyed your relationship once. Because you know she can't be everything to you either, even in all her fucking magnificence, because you're massive, you're immense. The elephant in this room is *you*, and just because you aren't fucking anyone else right now, doesn't mean she's all you'll ever need.

Silence.

SIMON

You think you know everything.

Silence.

CAMILLE

I only know what people are willing to tell me.

SIMON

Knowing and understanding aren't the same thing.

CAMILLE

All your philosophizing doesn't make you the wise one here.

Silence.

SIMON *closing up, tense*

If only you listened instead of losing it, over me differentiating—oh wait, sorry, *discriminating*, there, I've *exposed* myself as a sexist monster!—over me saying I'm scared. All you got out of it is: I'm totally fine with girls but guys terrify me?

CAMILLE *sucks in a breath*

Do you realize what you're saying? "Oh Camille, girls are no threat to me, come on, I'm the boyfriend, the primary, literally no vagina can measure up to the power of my penis!"

SIMON

That's not. What I. Am saying.

CAMILLE

It may not be what you meant, but it is what you said. Alice has three partners: Gayle, me and you. And when have you ever imagined she loves you more than she loves Gayle? More than she loves me? But now here you are, out of the blue, thinking she loves Eloy more than you? I knew you had quite the ego, but now you've just managed to obliterate anyone who isn't you. You think you love her *more* than *I* do?

Silence.

CAMILLE

You think he's going to make her come harder? That he's wittier than you? You think it doesn't bother *us* to see her swoon over him like she's falling in love for the first time? You think we *enjoy* seeing her bursting with NRE? Knowing that even though she still loves us, we're not the New Shiny anymore? If there were only women in her life, you think she'd be on the prowl for you? Or him? That she'd be missing a goddamn dick in her life?

Silence.

CAMILLE

You're whining because you imagine Eloy might be what Alice has always wanted. But don't forget, last time you tried having her all to yourself, she was totally capable of getting the fuck out of the relationship. Gayle loved Alice to death before you came begging for a second chance. She didn't have to give you one.

Simon holds his head in his hands.

CAMILLE

Your dick might be bigger than mine, Simon, but that doesn't give you the right to claim the place of alpha male.

unchosen family
(april)

simon

<u>and the baby with only one dad</u>

Alice's fingers are busy making a butterfly out of knots at the centre of my throat, over my Adam's apple.

If I got pregnant...

A bad start to a conversation. I want to interrupt, hush her by plastering a kiss on her mouth—

...would you want to do a paternity test?

She fiddles with my bowtie, the wool argyle-patterned one that's impossible to place properly. I'll be choking soon, when she tightens it, but at least her being so close to me gives me the chance to inhale her perfume, the Vanilla Fields she only uses on important occasions. She's leaning over me, over the bowtie, and I catch a glimpse of her black bra. Front closure. The clasp presses against her skin, digs in a bit. When she's taking it off tonight, she'll complain about the redness between her breasts.

I inhale a whiff of perfume before answering her question.

Whose it is would be obvious, eventually.

Maybe, but your mom won't want anything to do with the kid if she's not sure it's yours.

What can I say, she'll have to live with the mystery.

She'll want it baptized if it's yours.

We'll deal with my mom if and when you get pregnant, not before.

But I'm curious! I would love to see her face when she realizes it might not *be yours and* won't be baptized!

She makes a face, readjusting the inflexible fabric under the collar of my shirt.

Okay, look in the mirror, tell me what you think.

I turn to the mirror and Eloy appears behind me, framed by the door.

Gayle's ready. You coming?

A bad joke pops into my head. Making the verb *to come* into a dirty double-entendre isn't my style. He must be rubbing off on me.

Like all the mirrors in the house, this one is too low. I have to bend over to see myself and finish adjusting the bowtie. Alice left, and Eloy disappeared as quickly as he *came*. Heh heh.

I lean on the sink cabinet as though it would hold me up.

I imagine slapping my own face to pull myself together, find myself ridiculous and wind up sitting on the bed. We're getting ready to go to a funeral, I'm supposed to be sad, but I feel better with a knot *on* my throat than *in* it. Better dressed than naked.

I'm hooked. I don't know about him, but me? I think I'm in love. Things were falling into place, *we* were falling into place, then Camille said *okay, I'm done processing*, and things had to change again. You can't put yourself out there without putting yourself out there.

Now that he knows what sleeping with a guy is like, we have to work out the logistics again, as though he'd just moved in, except this time, the process isn't as clear.

It was just the one time, after all.

Do I have to define the relationship if I'm already in love

after this one time? I'm ridiculous. I thought my tension was jealousy, then desire. But I'm always this uptight. I only relaxed for the three seconds it took to ejaculate, long enough for my brain to register the sight of my come drenching his belly.

I get embarrassed just looking at him. In other words, I don't look at him much.

Before we slept together, I was fixated on the idea of him being better than me, ergo, logically, he wouldn't want me. Now, it's a done deal so, he wanted me enough for it to happen, or was at least curious enough to give plain-old-me a trial run. Once does not a habit make. If he doesn't want to do it again, let him tell me so. Let him prove me right.

I like being right.

I don't like it when there's no one to assure me of it.

My girlfriend's vanilla scent is lingering in my nostrils and it makes me absurdly happy.

Not that I don't find it useful to provoke my mom the way she has provoked—and will provoke—us, but her contrariness knows no limit. Using our family utopia to piss my mother off amuses Alice, but it's not helpful; I'm not trying to alienate my mother, I just don't want any Catholicism in my life.

Keeping all my families intact wouldn't be a bad thing.

Maybe having a kid of my own would bring us closer. Mom would rather be excommunicated than miss out on her grandchild growing up. Even if it meant putting up with my homosexual lovers and my "*peculiar* living arrangement," as she calls it.

I imagine the scent of Johnson & Johnson on a baby's skin and it makes me absurdly happy.

The half-smile reflected back in the mirror is out of character. I'm floating away, but I manage to stand up.

I'm going to have to drive, no doubt, even though I have no idea how to get to the funeral home. Alice makes a bad co-pilot, and she'll be busy doing damage control, what with Camille's uncontrollable grief. We'll get lost in the sketchy maze of east Sherbrooke. Oh well.

what was left unsaid

Near the front door, Gayle re-braids Camille's hair. Both of them already have their coats and boots on.

Eloy approaches to get his coat off the hook, puts it on, then goes around them both to put on his runners. When he bends over to tie them up, Camille starts to cry.

These two events are unrelated.

Gayle holds Camille and rubs her back.

Eloy stands back up, visibly uncomfortable. He puts his hand on Camille's shoulder. She stops crying.

Silence.

camille

and the Father, the "Son," and the Holy Grammie

I recognized the paternal household's number on the display. I don't know where Yves found my number, but I picked up before realizing it was a bad idea, it had to be bad news. And it was. He said *there's not a lot of ways to say this, Francine is dead,* then blathered on for ten minutes about *funeral planning* this and *calls to make* that, the *morgue* and *the coroner* and *blah blah blah.* She died alone at home. Cause as yet unknown.

She wasn't sick, it just happened.

He drones on. I'm not registering much—my grandmother just died, give me a second to digest, would you!?—until he says: *So, you're coming when?*

I say nothing while reviewing my list of potential responses:

Do I have to?

Who else will be there?

Can I bring the Family to face the family?

Is it snowing hard enough to excuse my absence?

I haven't seen him in six and a half years. I was just starting to believe that thinking about him wouldn't affect me.

Yves's place wasn't set up for a girl, for making a girl into a girl, I mean. His place was for making men. *Real* men. The living room smelled (probably still smells) of log cabin. No matter where you decided to sit, the stuffed deer were always looking right at you. A disturbing place. In the kitchen, everything was optimized for maximum domestic efficiency, so as to spend the least time there as possible: sharp knives, cutting boards bolted to the countertop. The basement was all about hunting. Rifles on the wall. Boxes of crossbow bolts. Ceiling equipped with rabbit hangers.

The house was supposed to reek of success—ours, to make up for his failures—but it smelled stale instead. The air was heavy with regrets, circulating in a house that was too small and too far out to measure up to his ambition.

I could have been a doctor! he used to say.

It smelled dank, but it wasn't supposed to. It wasn't the kind of atmosphere he wanted, or the kind we needed. He probably made us breathe that air so we could filter it. We were supposed to suck it in deep and only exhale it in a house dripping with luxury, or better yet, in a lavishly decorated office with a cornucopia-like salary, overflowing with hunting trips to Anticosti Island twice a year.

Chez Yves, the hope was, we would fill our pockets with money and masculinity.

I failed at both.

In my head, I quickly calculate the odds of a shouting match if I bring my little Family to his place. He's never even met Gayle, he might've met Alice once, but the guys, they're a problem. I can see it now, him pulling me aside and harassing me with questions: *Are you sleeping with them? Are they fags? You told me you like chicks (no Yves, yes Yves, yes Yves). Stop calling me*

Yves, I'm your dad for fuck sakes, I only want the best for you and if you hang out with fairies...

My father, the '50s-style bigot.

He likes his head in the sand. Especially when it comes to me.

According to him, being assigned male at birth and wanting to be reassigned female is like being homosexual, but a touch more fucked up. Even after hours of explaining patiently, emailing resources, and leaving brochures around the house, he still sees me as his son, only a half-assed one.

I should wear a nametag, just to see. "Hello, my name is Camille (for fuck sakes)."

Grammie was more modern than her son. She hid the princess dresses under the staircase and explained my preferences to my brother in the most heteronormative terms possible: *If you're the prince, someone has to be the princess, and it's sure not going to be me!*

Oh Grammie.

Couldn't you have stuck around a while longer?

Couldn't you have given me a heads-up?

Couldn't you have convinced your "little boy" that I'm the one who knows what's best for me?

When I finally managed to tear the receiver away from my ear, I started to cry. I sobbed as loud as I could so someone would come hold me tight in his arms, her arms, or all of the above.

Alice came into my room in a panic. I hiccupped out that Grammie was dead, she held me and rocked me for what seemed like hours. Eventually I stopped sobbing and she gently asked me questions: *Where do you have to go? What do you need? Who do you want with you? What do you want to wear?*

Gotta go to my dad's, I need a ride, I want everyone there, I don't just have a support person, *I have a support* system, *it's all four of you or no one at all, what am I going to wear?*

What the hell am I going to wear?

eloy

hates the telephone

It's not that I don't love my parents, I just have no interest in speaking to them.

Last week, Simon told me his mother would come by to drop off a toolbox she didn't want anymore—*I got myself a new one, it has everything, why don't you take the old one so you can stop calling your landlord every time your tap starts dripping*—and he asked me if I would be home to receive both mother and toolbox. He didn't need to ask, I never leave the house except for my usual Saturday coffee at Kàapeh Bistro, but whatever, I said I'd receive the delivery in question, thinking it must be nice to have parents close by like that.

My parents left Notre-Dame-du-Nord when my eldest sister, Roxane, was born. My father didn't want her baptized and apparently it was easier to leave than get their way, especially since my mother (both anglophone and Ontarian, two quasi-cancerous birthmarks in the eyes of NDDN inhabitants) was already the object of daily ridicule. Saint-Eustache is where Lee-Ann and I were born, and there, people didn't give a shit if we were baptized or not, as long as we didn't set the church on fire. When I left Sherbrooke to do my BA, my parents went back to Témiscamingue for their pre-retirement. My father got his pension, and a tent-trailer appeared in the yard. They're textbook Boomers. I see them once a year, at Christmas.

Gayle says we're supposed to do more, family-wise. Says who? I don't see why. She can set an example of "proper behaviour toward family" as much as she wants, I won't start calling them once a week, or seeing them more than once a year. They can call or write, if they need to talk. That's good enough for me.

When I got my sister's email that her girlfriend had given birth to their second child, I didn't drop everything to rush over there and play Uncle, and Alice was shocked. It doesn't take much.

Just before Simon's mother came by, I was considering whether to call them. I know Emily leaving me worried them, and they invited me to Ville-Marie for a few weeks (or months, or years). I maybe would have gone if I hadn't found plan B, but there's only so much you can ask from your parents. And now, with Camille's Grammie kicking the bucket, it's tough. I'm not close enough to her to help, but close enough to hurt. I don't know. I only know I feel like talking to my parents. I'm probably a cliché. Fuck.

When I met Simon's mother, I stopped envying him for having his parents nearby. She came in without knocking, holding a huge toolbox. I was alone in the living room with my laptop and the big cat was overflowing from my lap. I must have seemed dazed because she didn't say anything at first. When she saw me, she was still on the entry mat with the door open behind her, looking both rushed and annoyed. She stared at me like she was going to eat my soul. A tuft of hair hung in her eyes a little, and it was thinning, but that just amped up the whole effect. Her hairstyle scared me. I got up and the cat shoved off, complaining loudly.

Can I give you a hand?

Simon's not here?
No, he'll be back later tonight.
Would've been good if he'd let her know.
Well, where is he?
I don't know. You're his mom, I presume? He told me to tell you to leave the toolbox on the table.
The least he could do was be here to greet me himself.
Fuck.
I'll leave it here, then?
Yeah, that's good.
Ever get the urge to give the place a little vacuum?
Thanks for the tools.
Humph.

She left and my desire to speak to my parents had disappeared. I couldn't wait for Simon to get home so I could tell him his delivery management was for shit. Just because Alice puts up with her mother-in-law without a word, doesn't mean I will. He's already figured that out, by the way. I'm not an idiot, I'll be the nice guy as usual, but I won't let him subject me to her in our home, that's for sure.

I don't know at this point. About my parents. We're going to the funeral of a woman I've never met, we'll meet a bunch of sad people I'd rather not meet, and my parents would be far less stressful in comparison.

Seeing my number on their display will worry them, I call them so rarely. I could say I miss the forests of Témiscamingue. Or that looking for a job with an environmental studies diploma is like dying a slow death, even if you worked in marketing on the side for years. My parents remember Alice and probably think we are going to get back together. I don't know what I would tell them—*Actually mom, I'm more into her boyfriend, but I'm not saying no.* I could also tell them that my favourite roommate, the one I'm not attracted to but still consider my girlfriend somewhat, thinks I'm depressed, but *don't worry I'll be okay*, as long as I find a fucking job right fucking now, because I'm a total drag.

I'm useless without a job, and I'm not much use to begin with.

I'll say: *Can we get together? I'm tired. There's too much death around here right now.*

gayle's

mother isn't dead

I'm a bad person.

No, I'm not. I can't be, because I make the best apple pies in the whole universe, and apple pies are kindness made out of butter, right? Right.

I'd concocted a lasagna for supper, the kind of meal you only make for big occasions, making those bloody things takes such a long time. Luckily it turned out fucking delicious. I was serving myself a third helping when Camille said *I have to go see my father.*

No, that wasn't what she said. She implicated me.

She said *come with me. To see Yves.*

No.

I couldn't say the word, so like a good little coward, I said no indirectly. I stammered out a completely useless *uhhh, when?* I could hear me making fun of myself in my head—*She's going, okay? And she needs you, but you're way too spineless.*

My eyes have never been so glazed over. I couldn't see a thing.

I don't even like glaze.

She's going to start crying again. What am I supposed to do, besides give her a hug?

I've never grieved for anyone and I don't know what I'm

supposed to say. Maude told me about when she was in high school and her best friend's grandmother died. A teacher asked her friend if they were close. Apparently, she found it offensive, because she slapped his face and stomped out of the classroom. A story worthy of note, because the girl wasn't expelled. *It seems you can get away with anything, if people feel sorry for you*, Maude said.

I hadn't even heard of Camille's Grammie before yesterday. I don't understand why she's hurting so bad, but I can't ask her, I might get my face slapped. It's not that I don't like face slapping. I just prefer to be on the giving end; getting them isn't as nice. Except this slap would be a total fail. A slap from pissed-off Camille, not horny Camille.

In the end, Alice went with her to see him. She didn't want to risk bringing the guys along. They'll only come to the funeral.

Camille was well aware I wasn't capable of going—too chicken, as aforementioned—but it was Alice who said it'd be easier for me to stay behind, that I could do some housework while they were gone. I jumped on the chance. *I'll do the dishes, everything'll be all nice when you get back, you'll see.*

Before shutting the door, Camille said *could you wash the sheets? I need nice soft sheets.*

They're done now, I should go put them in the dryer actually, but I still have a pile of dishes to take care of. The water pooled in the sink is disgusting, the kind of disgusting that leaves a ring of grease on the stainless steel. I tried to drain it, but the sink's plugged. The water is draining at a trickle, I can feel a slight swirl when I put my hand over the hole, but it's not enough, with the tap spitting hot water. Which is fucking scalding hot instead of disgusting. I can't be bothered to adjust the temperature.

I wish I'd known my granny. Maybe then I would understand better what Camille expects of me.

The oldest person in my life is my seventy-year-old mother, a hard-core singleton. The hottest little old lady in Saint-Eustache—oh, wait, that's right, she's not single anymore, she met a gentleman, *very lovely and also very much my type, you'll see.* Not so old or hard core after all, my mom.

She always says we don't see each other enough—I don't have a licence and I hate the bus—but three or four visits a year is plenty. Suburbs pretending to be cities aren't my thing. I have no intention of going back to the boonies anytime soon.

Maybe if I had kids. But Saint-Eustache is out there; maybe mom would come live here instead.

I don't really want kids, to tell the truth. We already have a big Family: seven of us, for eff sakes, if you count the cats. The place is covered in human hair and cat hair. And all of us are already housebroken.

We were out of parchment paper so there's cookie dough stuck to the baking sheet. I'll soak it and wash it tomorrow morning. Worst-case scenario, they'll bug me about it, best-case, no one will say a thing. Now that Camille is grieving, nobody's nagging. So what's supposed to get me to do chores?

I would want Camille to be the mother of my children anyway, and she can't anymore, unless she stops taking hormones for like, a year, and even then, there are no guarantees. While I'm at it, I'd like to send my regards to her endocrinologist, who somehow didn't think to mention the possibility of freezing some sperm *before* starting hormones, the genius.

Even if we adopt, in five years' time, say—a relatively realistic plan—mom will be seventy-five.

My dad's mom was that age when she died.

I can't even deal with the thought of our cats dying some-day, let alone my mother....

Now that I'm thinking about it, maybe it's better not to risk having kids if I'm about to lose my mom?

alice

is afraid of other families

I dreamed of Camille's grandmother, sitting up in her coffin during the funeral service, pointing at us and proclaiming *Sinners have no place in the house of God!*

That pretty much sums up the situation.

There was no debate. When a grieving person asks you to go somewhere, you go, even knowing full-well your being there might make things more awkward. So, we're going as a group, as a Family. The very idea of having to answer the question *so, how do you know, um...it's* Camille *now, is it?* makes me want to barf. I'm not sure "how we know each other" is something one shares. And *we're housemates* doesn't exactly cover it.

So now, I'm holding everyone up. I know they're waiting for me. I'm just going to sit on my bed here a sec, petting the big cat from a safe distance so as not to get any fur on my black dress.

I didn't tell my "roomies" I was uneasy. I never do and they can always tell anyway. I'm in danger of blowing up in the car, telling Camille I can't do it, that I'm not ready to put myself on display, to put *all of us* on display, in a quasi-holy place in front of a bunch of boring people and an overly perfumed corpse. If I scream *You know we're about to get stoned to death, right?!* it might be enough to make them change tack. No doubt it would be a completely inappropriate way to tell them that I'm nervous but frankly, I don't see how I could say it any other way.

Here's a (non-exhaustive) list of things people might say to us:

Is that like a cult?

Oh, you're in a commune! I heard about those when I was in California back in '76.

What? Polygamy?

Do you all sleep in the same bed?

Do you have, like, orgies and stuff?

There's five *of you? I can't even manage to keep* one!

What are you going to tell your kids?

I can't very well just answer *funnily enough, we were just talking about that!*

If we get there late and leave early, maybe no one will talk to us. That would be ideal.

There are reasons why you don't do that. Why that isn't done. Why I have never even told my own parents, even though technically it's me who started this whole thing years ago—apparently, I have a knack for converting followers to join my cult. And yet, there's something still a bit traditional about my family. And there's only five of us: three times fewer than the number of children my grandmother had!

This isn't the first family occasion we've faced, of course. But up to now, we've expertly avoided them. Or we've played the couples game (Gayle with Camille; Simon with me). We make up excuses as needed: the Christmas snowstorm; the work seminar that coincides with a sister's birthday; the *you know very well I don't celebrate Easter!* over the phone. If we didn't, people would start asking when we're getting married, when are we buying a house, when are we having kids.

Ideal scenario, no one would set foot in our house and we'd never go anywhere.

Simon will figure out I'm stalling soon. Gayle will be the one sent to get me, my no-bullshit girl.

To escape family drama when I was little, I would go into the closet used for storing off-season clothes and arrange the boxes to hide behind them. If someone opened the door, they'd only see cardboard. I would read by flashlight until I fell asleep.

When Mom discovered my hiding place, I burst into tears. She was so angry about being fooled so easily, she slapped my face. Full-on, her whole hand on my cheek. I stopped crying. She looked horrified (and never did it again, incidentally).

If I open the window wide, then hide under the bed, they'll think I jumped ship. They won't believe the cowardice, but still.

It would work, if only this weren't the fifth floor.

If Gayle were to catch me as I slipped under the bed, she would definitely say what I need to hear—*What the hell are you doing?! We're all waiting for you!*—and I would follow her in tears, because I'm just as afraid of getting my face slapped now as I was at nine and a half.

And besides, if I did hide under the bed, my dress would get covered in cat hair.

I have to go.

Getting slapped by all of them—now that would really sting.

temporary arrangement—the rerun

(not quite july)

alice

<u>doesn't ask questions</u>

You said you were leaving, and no one said much.

You didn't make an announcement, not even *I've got something to tell you.* No, you just said it between mouthfuls of chili: *I got the job with the City, in Ville-Marie. I leave Friday.*

Way out in Ville-Marie, regional county municipality of Abitibi-Témiscamingue, Quebec.

I mean, do they even have Wi-Fi there?

You said you were leaving, and Gayle nodded and smiled at you. You didn't look at anyone else at first, probably knowing she'd react the least. Not that she isn't attached to you, but everyone knows she has a talent for going with the flow. You "looked" at her the way you do, which is to say by first looking at her plate, then at the wall, then at her forehead, then at her eyes for maybe a fraction of a second; but this time, a bit like when you're mad and completely avoid eye contact, you were staring at a spot on her face. You were looking at her cheek. No, you were looking *through* it.

She was still smiling when Camille blurted out: *Is it good money, at least?*

You turned toward her, running your fingers through your hair in a futile attempt to push it away from your glasses.

Twenty-five an hour.

Everyone *ooh*ed and *aah*ed admiringly.

I grabbed Simon's poor little hand, so tightly clenched on his lap. He hardly reacted to my fingers wrapping around his, might not have even felt it. You turned to me, but I avoided your gaze. I think you wanted to know if Simon was okay, but I didn't feel like being your go-between.

Are you even wondering how *I* am?

The thing with Simon is, when something happens, he sulks for three days before being able to verbalize discomfort or frustration or sadness. That's a long time, three days, but it's like clockwork; once he starts looking sullen and speaking in monosyllables, there's no point trying to get anything out of him until seventy-two hours have elapsed.

So, I held his hand and silently started the countdown: *71 hours, 59 minutes, 59 seconds.*

I review all the times you could have mentioned wanting to move so far away and realize that, even after you and Simon started Frenching full-time, you never said you wouldn't leave, which for you was probably tantamount to a warning. You'll disengage, you'll say we shouldn't have. Is feeling useless in Sherbrooke worse than feeling lonely in Ville-Marie? You never asked yourself that, I'll bet. You believe we'll be better off without you because you're broke, and you won't let us support you. We're not done with you, you know. You're leaving before we're done.

Where are you going to live?
Dunno.
How are you getting there?
Dunno.
How long are you staying?
Dunno.
Are you going alone?
Dunno.

I had other questions, so many others, but my voice would've cracked, and I didn't want that. I kept my mouth firmly shut and looked down so you wouldn't see the tears welling up in my eyes. I had no idea if it was hard for you too, because it didn't show, it never does, you just sat there like you do, making it look like you're fine. You don't even make a sound. We just have to guess and that's that.

But I needed you to talk to me.

Are you happy?

Dunno.

The questions I ask aren't the right ones. I could write a lengthy list of relevant questions that will never be part of this conversation:

Did you actually want to live with us?

Do you think I forced you into staying so long?

Did you like it here?

Would you rather stay?

Do you love me? Do you love us?

And if I said I loved you, how would you feel?

And if we said we loved you, how would you feel?

gayle

You're doing things backwards, sweetie. You should take off for the *winter*, flying south like the birds. Not now, when the tulips are wilted but the apple trees haven't bloomed yet. You have terrible timing.

You set the table, and that's it. Now you expect us to put dinner on it. But I've lost my appetite.

I'm probably smiling as I look at you. It's not because I don't give a shit, you know. It's just my way. When there's trouble, I either smile or start cooking like mad, but we're already eating. I could make a dessert, but we have no milk or eggs. What am I supposed to do with that? With*out* that?

Newsflash: the others thought you'd stay. In their pretty little heads, your *it's just temporary* was bullshit. The others are imagining what you might say. They have to, you aren't talking. If you did, we wouldn't have to provide the script, something to remind ourselves that you're more than just a funny guy with a pretty face. You actually have feelings. I imagine.

I don't know how anyone could get attached to someone like you. What can I say? It happened. I didn't put any particular effort into getting, or *not* getting, attached. I was just here at the same time as you, with my cookies and my cats, and that was all it took.

You always say you're difficult and hate people, but that can't be true, otherwise you wouldn't love *us*.

But you don't say it, you would never say *I love you all*. Even saying *I'm a vegetarian* would be too much of a commitment.

Who's going to do the dishes now when it's my turn to cook? Fuck. I never knew I needed a henchman until I had one.

You brought the silence with you, it slipped in here along with your garbage bags full of faded clothes, but it didn't really settle in until Camille's grief made room for it. Now that it has space to expand, it comes more easily. Like right now. The silence. It's not peaceful. It's oppressive.

No one seems to have anything to add. I'm getting used to the silence. Before you came, I would have tried to fill it.

Is that what you came here to teach me, honeybun? Is that your legacy?

Hang on a sec, sorry, you aren't dead—yet—and here I am, talking like I'll never see your face again.

How far is Ville-Marie?

There. I broke the silence. Couldn't help myself.

From Sherbrooke? Nine hours, non-stop.

camille

had no clue

I didn't even know you had an interview. When you said you were going to Ville-Marie for the weekend, I thought it was to visit your own grandmother. That my mourning had made you nostalgic.

Didn't you get the urge to tell me? It's simple enough, *I have an interview*. See? Even I can put that sentence together. Maybe I'm not important enough. We're not sleeping together, we're not all gaga over each other, so you don't owe me anything, we have nothing to say to each other. And yet, I'm the one you talk to. I'm the one who asks you the right questions. If we were in grade five, you'd call me your "best friend."

I'm not your roomie, not yet your lover.

I didn't think you were the type to go back to your hometown. Saying Témiscamingue is too small for you wouldn't make much sense, geographically speaking. But I do wonder if you'll find anyone like you there. Not physically, of course—I'm sure you'll find other cis-white men of Catholic descent there. What I mean is, people like *us*.

But wait. Do you consider yourself bisexual now? Pansexual? Does it even matter to you? Are you well known in Ville-Marie? Would it scare you if I came to visit sporting a five o'clock shadow? Okay, so they didn't stone us at the funeral home, but in Témiscamingue? Who knows what they'll do.

The way you're staring at Gayle scares me. Everyone knows I'm not the jealous type, it's that what you're looking for is her approval. As though you know that finding absolution in her pretty gaze would mean a pardon from everyone else and then you won't have to suffer anymore, right?

Stop it. Suck it up, buttercup.

Subjecting me to your NRE and how irritatingly sappy you made each of them wasn't enough. No, you had to go and leave, dumping me in the middle of the inevitable slump to follow. I wish I hadn't encouraged you to get close to them. Now I have to go through everyone being down in the dumps for the next six months. This was doomed from the start.

Your little speech is of no concern to me. We all stopped talking to leave space for you—you don't take up much as it is, just the bare minimum—except you won't add anything relevant. Anything relevant you could say isn't something you say. Such as:

I did say it was temporary.

I couldn't find anything in Sherbrooke, that's why I had to look so far away.

I don't think I'll be back, even on vacation.

I'm sorry.

An *I'm sorry* to all of us would be in order, in fact, but it would probably make me want to wind up and slap you.

I'm hot, Eloy, so hot. Pour your glass of water over my head. We were supposed to stick together in this apartment full of dumbasses. You were meant to bring me a little respite, help me create a peaceful vibe, something no one else can do because of *feelings.*

We embody indifference, you and I. The thing that provides a break. We love quietly, did you know that?

I love you quietly.

simon

<u>is left for dead</u>

Since you got back from your interview—exactly seven days ago—I've been fantasizing about sliding up behind you at your desk, ripping off your headphones, and hurling your computer out the window.

I would get off on hearing the zombie screams in your speakers fading out until your computer hits the pavement.

So much gratuitous violence.

It was no use asking you *what're you gonna do if you get the job?* every fucking day. You were incapable of answering. You needed to kill all the living dead on your screen first instead, so you applied yourself to the task with all the tenacity I know you have in you. That we all know you have.

Oh wait, *now* I get it.

I'm the one Left 4 Dead!

(Good one. Very funny.)

You're sitting in front of me, we're surrounded by our loves as well as our love, yours and mine. And tonight like every night, at every dinnertime, you don't look me in the eye.

Monday morning, you told me I'd been grinding my teeth during the night. I was dreaming of zombies. I dreamed you were leaving to live with them so you could study them in their natural habitat, like Jane Goodall and the chimpanzees—or was it Dian Fossey with the gorillas? I'm not quite sure which. I've never been sure, actually. You were traversing Québec on foot, groaning (you had to imitate them to be accepted as one of them). You were moving them to Opemican National Park, south of Ville-Marie, so you could convert them to deer brains. You kept yelling *braaiiins* to lure them in the right direction. You were mixing human and deer brains together.

Hm. You must have mentioned that park at some point. How else would it show up in my dream? Why else would I dream of anything in the vicinity of Ville-Marie?

Are you talking to me? I can't hear you over the sound of zombies groaning in my head.

I Googled "Ville-Marie" that afternoon. It's on the shore of Lake Témiscamingue, near Ontario. The Algonquin name for the place is Wikwedo. The 2006 census counted 2,696 inhabitants. It's the most populous city in the region of Témiscamingue.

Wow. Doesn't take much to be considered "populous" out there.

I've often thought we had too many people per square foot in here. You took up such a small amount of space. You never really settled in. Never mentioned repainting your room. Never hung anything on the walls. There were curtains already. *They're ugly, but dark. And curtains are expensive.*

If we'd wound up sharing a room, my obsession with cleaning and decorating would have driven you crazy. I would have loved that. I would have put up blinds and dazzled you by opening them while you were still asleep. I would have followed you around the room while you were undressing so I could pick up the clothes in your wake.

I don't think you knew what you were getting yourself into when we became friends, much less when we became lovers. But since I can't put my finger on exactly when we became *something*, how could I warn you?

I'm amazed that you stayed within these walls for so long—your walls, our walls.

I've slept in your arms almost every night since the spring and you still make me queasy. Ten months of proximity nausea. Maybe that's why you're leaving, to spare us. Or just to spare me.

I don't know how to love you without hurting myself. I've even gotten really good at that. It's all I know how to do.

Not long ago, I told myself that if I didn't admit my love to you, I could keep you for myself, that I could love and admire you longer by keeping it to myself, by giving you all the space you wanted and never asking anything of you. That way our love would be like a novel, the kind Alice loves so much, the ones featuring monogamous bliss and many children.

Maybe monogamous love is the best kind of love, since it's everywhere.

(I'm so funny. A real fucking riot.)

You hate being looked at, being seen, and right now I'm staring at you, my love, laying you bare, laying you out here, in our kitchen, as though it were a public event like a funeral or a wedding. You're drowning in denial. It's like the lid of your coffin staying shut—no one knows you're in there, so you're safe. For now.

We're both safe, and so is everyone around us. We just have to let things be.

Maybe I should be sad, but I'm not. I'm not even feeling sorry for myself, can you tell? Can you all tell?

But no, even *you* think I'm trying to create future drama by keeping everything inside, by not telling you *exactly* how I feel.

Can you tell me how to make you stay forever? Tell me now.

eloy

isn't putting bread on the table

This was just temporary. Did I ever say that out loud, or did I just think it? Because yeah, I expected a weird reaction, but not this complete silence. Tumbleweeds are rolling by. You can hear crickets chirping. But it's just the sound of cat claws on the fake wood flooring.

Oh shit, the cats. I was trying not to think about them.

Would You hold it against me for using my family contacts to find a job because I couldn't find one even after looking everywhere in Quebec? Probably not, knowing You. You'd be happy for me, after the initial disappointment.

There's nothing here for me but You. And polyamory? Well, it doesn't put bread on the table.

I hear Your objections: *We could've supported you!*

Even your voices get mixed up in my head. I can't tell them apart anymore, which should worry me. And yet You aren't a single entity. You all know what you want, that's all.

As for what *I* want, maybe I should have made that more clear. But as You know, I don't go on about my feelings.

I want to do something with my life. It's important.

The first time we all had a meal together, You were a closed-off unit. Since I was completely closed off as well, we could have gone along like that for quite a while. It was perfect, it could have stayed perfect. Okay, You wanted to love me, and I wound up loving You back, so fine, wow, we're all symbiotic and shit. But it's not perfect. You took a risk. I don't integrate, I won't integrate. I'm closing off again because You need company and me, I'm not fit for company.

I'm not looking forward to You asking if I'll be coming back soon. If my leaving You behind means I'm leaving You. It's just a physical separation, after all. Am I bad at maintaining relationships? Yes. Do I want to maintain this? Well, "maintain" is a shitty word for it. You'll see, once I come up with a better one.

You're thinking about the future, I can see it in Your eyes. It would be best if I left right away. If only I could. It'd be better, way better. Then they could say *he disappeared like a sweet potato in chili*. Copyright yours truly.

In a minute, I'll get up, rinse my plate, and go back to my room. You'll watch me go, eager for me to be out of earshot so You can say who knows what about me (about *You*, about *us*).

You'll all wonder if I'll eventually come back.

No one will have any idea.

what's moving

The patch of grass in front of the apartment building. New leaves on the oak trees on either side of the drive.

Constant drizzle and wind.

Camille pushes the door to the building open with her foot. She carries a big box over to Eloy's VW parked out front, where Simon is busy re-arranging—for the third time in thirty minutes—boxes that were carelessly shoved in earlier.

Gayle is lying on the hood, leaning back against the windshield with her eyes closed. If the sun was out, you'd think she was tanning.

SIMON *to Camille as she approaches*
> There's no more room!

GAYLE *turning toward them*
> You told her that three boxes ago.

CAMILLE
> Those tweakers upstairs said to tell you to leave them in the driveway. We'll put them on the seats just before he leaves.

SIMON
> It's raining you know.

GAYLE *face turned to the sky, eyes closed again*
> Apparently.

CAMILLE
> I told them that, but I don't make the decisions.

Simon sighs.

Camille puts the box down on the sidewalk and surveys the Tetris game in progress.

She picks up one of the boxes he put back on the street and puts it on top of a stack inside the car.

Simon glares at her, puts the box back on the ground and chooses another, smaller box to replace it with.

Camille opens the passenger-side back door and takes a seat.

Silence.

Simon finishes his Tetris game and joins Camille on the back seat.

Gayle calmly gets up and stretches. She jumps off the hood and gets in behind the wheel.

Silence.

Camille gently massages Gayle's shoulders. Simon looks out the window.

It starts to rain harder.

GAYLE
> We should just take off.

CAMILLE
> With all his stuff?

GAYLE
>Why not?

CAMILLE
>His clothes are hideous.

SIMON
>They're not so bad.

Camille and Gayle stare at him, frozen in shock. He shrugs.

Silence.

The windows fog up.

Camille resumes massaging Gayle. Simon goes back to staring out the window.

SIMON
>They're here.

Alice and Eloy run toward the car, each carrying a stuffed garbage bag. Alice opens the back door, tosses her bag into their laps then gets in beside Camille. Eloy takes the passenger seat.

Their doors slam at the same time.

Silence.

ELOY *looking ahead*
>So, you're all coming?

Silence.

GAYLE *whining*
>It's so far away.

ELOY
No one forced you to be here.

CAMILLE
It was raining.

Silence.

CAMILLE *whispering*
It's still raining.

Silence.

The rain intensifies until the noise is deafening.

Simon reaches out for Alice's hand. Their hands are on the garbage bag, the bag is on Camille's legs, Camille's legs are on the seat...and the branch was on the tree and the tree was in the ground, and the green grass grew all around, all around.

SIMON
I'm tired.

CAMILLE
You brought like, *two* boxes down.

SIMON
Hey, I lifted tons of them!

GAYLE
Unnecessarily.

A beat.

ALICE
I should've ordered pizza.

GAYLE

I'm craving falafels.

CAMILLE

The Beirut's too far.

GAYLE

But I'm starving!

SIMON

There's not enough time.

ELOY

Indeed.

Silence.

ELOY

You can go once I've left.

A long silence.

GAYLE

You forget, I'm the one behind the wheel.

ELOY

You have no licence, as far as I know?

SIMON

That's it. Today we die.

GAYLE

I'm really not that bad!

ALICE

It's a standard, honey.

Camille snorts.

GAYLE *acting offended*
> What could go wrong?

Silence.

The rain lightens up.

ELOY
> I've gotta get going.

GAYLE
> Okay.

Silence.

CAMILLE
> Okay, so…

ALICE
> Message when you get there, okay?

ELOY
> I'll be okay, you know.

ALICE
> Do it anyways.

He sighs.

ELOY
> Fine.

Silence.

GAYLE
> See you soon.

ELOY
     Um. Sure.

A long silence.

Eloy opens his door.

ELOY
     Okay, bye then.

Simon starts to cry.

Eloy turns to look at Alice, Camille and Simon.

CAMILLE
     Group hug?

Simon sniffles, smiling.

Eloy sighs.

ELOY *also smiling*
     Fine!

They wrap arms around each other, including the front seats in their hug. Alice bends to kiss each of their foreheads in turn.

Eloy sighs again, motions to Gayle to change seats. They go out and around and get back in.

Silence.

He puts the key in the ignition but doesn't turn it.

ELOY
     You know you're all still in my car, eh?

Translator's Note

I was once asked how I translate a book. As I started musing on my answer, pondering the internal workings of trans-creating a reading experience from one language to another, he went on to ask what computer program did I feed the text into, something like Google Translate? "No," I said, "I do it myself. It's all in my head." "But how...oh, do you speak Italian?" he asked.

"Yes, I speak Italian."

His question raised a common misunderstanding about the task of translating—speaking the language is necessary, but that is just the first and most basic step. The specific challenge for a literary translator is to go beyond the literal meanings of the work to preserve the deeper nuances and intentions of the author. It also involves devising creative solutions for bridging differences between languages and cultures.

The Fifth presented unique challenges in this respect. Not only was bridging required between Québecois French and English, certain subcultures are also involved—queer and polyamorous—each with distinct lingo in each language.

Idioms and humour present particular challenges, never more so than when humour hinges on an idiom. One notable example of this was the Québecois expression "avoir les yeux dans la graisse de bines" which literally translates as "having eyes in the bean fat" and refers to looking spaced out.

I couldn't use that expression because the humour hinged on the reference to beans: the character quips that she doesn't even like beans. The solution was to find an English idiomatic equivalent involving food—preferably pastry, in keeping with the character's love of baking. "Eyes glazed over" was my final choice because it allowed me to pivot on the multiple meanings of "glaze." Another example is the original subtitle (*roman d'amours*) which gives a polyamorous spin on the "romance" genre by pluralizing it (literally "romances"). I decided that subverting the iconic *Love Story* (Erich Segal's 1970s book, adapted to film) to *a love(s) story* was the best way to reproduce the humorous effect of the original.

The many grammatical differences between English and French are another area requiring bridging.

French has grammatical gender while English does not, presenting particular challenges when translating a queer novel. Also, French has different pronouns for *you* referring to a single person, versus *you* when referring to multiple people. And, there are different pronouns used for *we* equals "me and you," versus *we* equals "me plus multiple others." English's lack of these distinctions presents unique challenges when translating a polyamorous novel.

One particular conundrum of note hinged on gendered pronouns. Certain characters use the alternative plural pronoun *illes*—a combination of the masculine-plural *ils*, and the feminine-plural *elles*. I wasn't able to convey the significance of them using that pronoun (being that those characters are respectfully gender-sensitive) because English has yet to propose a nonbinary *plural* pronoun. The commonly used gender-inclusive *he/she* was of no use, because it is singular and it reinforces binary concepts of gender while the intention of *illes* is nonbinary. What's more, the nonbinary singular pronoun *they* appears identical to the plural pronoun *they*. Apart from being a fact leading to much consternation and debate, it leaves a translator with few options for respecting a gender-aware French text.

Since the characters' use of *illes* was an important aspect of characterization and of the novel's overall gender inclusivity, I explored various solutions for retaining both. One was to use singular nonbinary pronouns elsewhere in the novel (such as *zie*) but the characters didn't use their French equivalents (such as *iel* or *ille*). Another possibility was to coin a nonbinary plural pronoun. In order to avoid any awkwardness or disloyalty to the original text, I eventually decided to use plural they and capture what was lost using this note.

Solving the language puzzles in this translation was a delight. In my linguistic utopia, English writers would adopt a new nonbinary pronoun to refer to more than one person. I'm going to go brainstorm one now.

mp boisvert

With a master's degree in creative writing from the University of Sherbrooke, MP Boisvert is interested in the representation of polyamory in Quebec literature and issues of sexual diversity. MP Boisvert was Executive Director of the Quebec LGBT Council (2015–2020) and consultant for various Quebec and Canadian ministries on issues of sexual and gender diversity. She is the co-founder of Fière la fête!, Sherbrooke's Pride (QC).

Her contributions to *Zodiaque* (La Mèche, 2019), *Québe-Queer* (Les Presses de l'Université de Montréal, 2020), the academic journals *Cavale*, *Le Pied* and *Caractère*, as well as columns and articles on the blog "Littéraires après tout" and on the Fugues website, testify to a lively, daring and unique writing. Her first novel, *Au 5e*, published by Éditions La Mèche in 2017, deals with the intimacy of love experienced between five roommates.

monica meneghetti

Monica Meneghetti's first book, *What the Mouth Wants: A Memoir of Food, Love and Belonging* (Dagger Editions, 2017) was a Lambda Literary Award finalist and tied as the Bi Book Award winner. The book speaks to an array of open-minded readers, from foodies to relationship anarchists. Her translation from Italian, *The Call of the Ice: Climbing 8000-meter Peaks in Winter* (Mountaineers Books) was a Banff Mountain Book Award finalist. Her essay about being a queer child of Italian immigrants is found in *The Globe and Mail*. Her poetry, fiction and nonfiction appear in print, online, in musical scores, and on stage.

Meneghetti offers writing instruction and manuscript development services, with a focus on supporting marginalized voices. She lives with two of her three partners on unceded Coast Salish territories (Vancouver).